Which is correct?

Is the correct name Neanderthal or is it Neandertal?

The first find of a Neanderthal – Neandertal - fossil was discovered in 1856 in the Neander Valley in Germany. At that time (1856) the German word for valley was "Thal."

However, in 1904 Germany changed the spelling of their words to more closely resemble the "modern" pronunciation of their language. Consequently, THAL as in Neanderthal was changed to "TAL" as in Neandertal.

In Germany, and in most of Europe, the most popular spelling is Neandertal. In England and in the USA, the most frequently used spelling is Neanderthal.

Other books by
Edward F. Wagner

The Second People – (the beginning)
The first book in this series
ISBN 0-9679422-0-9

The Odyssey of The Second People
The second book in this series
ISBN 0-9679422-1-7

The Great Adventure of The Second People
The third book in this series
ISBN 0-9679422-2-5

They can still be ordered directly at www.wagnerpublishing.com

Edward F. Wagner

Ed Wagner is a native of Upstate New York. He and his family can trace their roots in the Albany, Schenectady, Troy, Amsterdam and Saratoga area along with Bennington and Rutland, Vermont for more than 200 years. His ancestors served their country in the Civil War and most of the major wars fought since then.

He grew up in Niskayuna where he graduated from Van Antwerp Junior High in 1953 and from the former Nott Terrace High School in Schenectady in 1956. He is also a graduate from SUNY Cobleskill (1958) where he majored in business. He served in the U.S. Army in the late 50's and early 60's as a combat engineer, specializing in atomic demolitions.

He is married to the former Joan Lawrence of Niskayuna and they currently reside in Clifton Park. They have six children and numerous grandchildren. His first-born grandson – Jared Doyle – is hidden in the foliage on the cover of his first novel.

Ed and Joan are Co-Managers of the Saratoga Springs Federal Credit Union, located at 480 Broadway in Saratoga Springs, NY.

He has been an avid outdoorsman for years and has many trophy whitetail bucks to his credit. His prize 16-point buck was taken in the region of Keene Valley in Essex County, NY. Many of the tracking secrets and hunting lore written in the books are from his personal experiences and knowledge of hunting, tracking and survival.

Ed is avidly interested in the study of early man, primarily the Neanderthal population of the Middle East region and Eastern Europe. He has read everything he can find on the newest and most startling discoveries concerning these peoples. Many of the discoveries, through 2003, are included in this 4th book of the series. Further discoveries will be incorporated into the 5th book (planed for 2005) and the 6th book that is planed for 2007.

He has been involved in writing a series of books using the Neanderthals, and the interaction between them and the Cro-Magnon peoples (also known as "Modern Man" in some places) as a central part of his fictionalized adventure romance stories. The first book was started in 1993 and was called "THE SECOND PEOPLE – the beginning." All the books in the planned six book series are based on scientific discoveries, but are written as thrilling adventure/romance fiction. All the books in the series will incorporate the phrase "The Second People" within the title.

DEDICATION

This 4th book in The Second People series is dedicated to the individuals who will in the future – perhaps as soon as six months from now or maybe six years or sixteen years from now – uncover a previously unknown site, or discover a new cave, or find a new tool, that shows beyond a shadow of a doubt that the people we refer to as Neanderthals were just as intelligent, resourceful, adventurous and adaptable as the new peoples (Cro-Magnon) that moved into their home regions.

It is now nearly universally accepted that the Neanderthals could speak and had language comparable to anyone else alive back then. Plus they cared for their sick, elderly and infirm as evidenced by the many skeletons unearthed that showed severe injury, deformities, and the infirmities of old age.

Announcements are being made, based on newly discovered findings from the regions of Eastern Europe, that were formally not available to paleontologists and anthropologists from the western countries. Discoveries seem to point to the Neanderthals having musical instruments; being able to attach spear points to shafts using a form of tar made out of pine pitch; and perhaps a glimmer of art in the form of cave drawings and/or carvings.

In the final few days of 2003, many individuals have made major announcements concerning Neanderthals and their culture.

Jean-Claude Marquet, curator of the Museum of Prehistory Grand-Pressigny, and Michel Lorblanchet, a director of research in the French National Centre of Scientific Research, Rocdes Monges @ Saint-Sozy, described a mask found at an excavation of a Paleolithic cave encampment as a Neanderthal mask carved out of stone. This announcement concerning the mask, as being made by Neanderthals was based on the tools and other artifacts found at the site that were Neanderthal. The experts called the 7.5-centimeter long bone and flint fragment mask a proto-figurine.

Clive Gamble from Southampton University, an expert on early occupation of Europe by human species says, and I quote "The great problem with the Neanderthal art is that they are one of's. With Neanderthals, there may have been the odd maker of art, but not repeated many times as with modern man's artwork."

Paul Bahn, a British expert on rock art, said, quote "It should finally nail the lie that Neanderthal's had no art. It is an enormously important object." He went on to say, "There are now a great many Neanderthal art objects. They have been found for decades and always have been dismissed."

Ivor Jankovic, of the Institute for Anthropological Research in Zagred, Croatia, speaking about the newest skull and other remains from Vindija, Croatia, which were dated to roughly 42,000 years ago, feels that the more delicate or "classic" bone structure suggests that the Neanderthals were interbreeding with modern humans in the region and thus moderating their appearance. He noted that the skull's supraorbital torus - - an arching, bony ridge above the eyes - - is not as thick and not as projecting as in other Neanderthal remains. The specimen skull also has a higher braincase than is typical in Neanderthals.

Dr. James Ahern, of the University of Wyoming says, and this is a direct quote "There was a far more complex dynamic going on between 20,000 years ago and 29,000 years than some people think. I'm sure that there were some things post-Neanderthal populations assimilated from their predecessors, certainly in the biological sense," Dr. Ahern told the BBC.

PREFACE

There are new discoveries and findings concerning the Neanderthals in Europe and also the Middle East nearly every month. Many of the most startling discoveries have come from the regions of Eastern Europe. It is in this area that new sites are being discovered. Astonishing new discoveries are changing the way that Neanderthals have been portrayed for generations.

Two individuals are in the forefront of changing the beliefs as to the ways Neanderthals lived and existed. They are Eric Trinkaus (Washington University in St. Louis) and Kharlena Maria Ramanan (Indiana State University). I have embraced their findings and beliefs and incorporated the newest and most startling finds (theirs and others) into this book.

This fourth book, in the planned six book series on primitive man incorporates into the storyline the following new and amazing discoveries concerning Neanderthals and their "humanism."

Flute made from the thighbone of a bear found in a Neanderthal cave site in Slovenia dated to between 43,000 years ago and 82,000 years ago.

The body of a four-year-old child who died about 25,000 years ago in a cave in Abrigo do Lagar Velho, Portugal that has definite mixture of Neanderthal and Cro-Magnon (modern man) traits and characteristics. Consequently he, or perhaps she, seems to have been the child of both Neanderthals and non-Neanderthal parents.

Both Neanderthals and "anatomically modern humans" lived side by side in the region known as THE LEVANT, from about 100,000 years ago up to roughly 40,000 years ago and shared the same culture.

The Neanderthals practiced specialized hunting and not random catch- as- catch can techniques. In and around the area of the Danube River there are two large sites, one around the plateau of Erd and the second around Tata. The sites give positive proof that the Neanderthals of the region practiced hunting that was planned and not just opportunistic. During the two or three months of early spring they concentrated on newly born and one year old cave bears. However, they also hunted horses, rhinos, deer, asses (donkeys), bovids (wild cattle) and young mammoths.

Neanderthal sites in the Russian regions of Moldova dated to roughly 42,000 years ago show that they were making shelters out of wood covered with animal skins.

Newly discovered Neanderthal bones, along with bone and stone tools in and around the Croatian region of Europe, have placed Neanderthals still living there to a period of about 35,000 years ago.

In the Vindija area, Neanderthals were beginning to show lower jaws featuring the beginnings of a pronounced chin, which would be a definite change in their physical appearance. Was this change due to interbreeding?

Neanderthal tools recently found in Europe indicate that the Neanderthals not only were making stone- tipped spears but attaching them to the wooden shafts using an adhesive made from birch pitch. Researchers in Germany have said that the adhesive is surprisingly good and very sophisticated in the process.

A tent-like structure, found in the Grotte du Lazaret near Nice, France, was inside a cave and made of animal hides draped over a wooden framework. It has been estimated that it is well over 100,000 years old and consequently had to have been made by Neanderthals.

The Neanderthal brain was about 13% larger (yes, larger!) than our own modern brain. The average height of Neanderthal men is estimated to be about five foot five inches and the Neanderthal females about five feet. Their joints and bones were thicker and larger and they had well muscled chests. Examining the places where the muscle attaches to bones it has been illustrated that their calves and biceps were extremely well developed, as were their pectoral chest and back muscles.

Neanderthal fossil remains have been found which indicate they definitely had the ability to talk.

Neanderthal's also cared for their sick and elderly as evidenced in many cave excavations.

In just the last few days of 2003, a few new discoveries concerning Neanderthals and art were announced.

I do want to apologize to those who are "purists" in the use of language. In my dialogs between people in the story, I do not use what would be grammatically correct words and phrases all the time. I also do not use the currently "politically correct," words. I think of how they would have talked 40,000 years ago and use that phraseology and grammar in the story.

1

Fawn sat down and looked at Lynx. Had she heard what had been said correctly? Her gaze shifted over to Gesher and then Ibex. Could it really be that she and the people that called themselves The Chosen were The First People?

Ibex stood next to Gesher and took his hand in hers. "Perhaps it would be good for us to go and take a walk. I want to hear more about the tales of The Second People that you know so that I can compare them to the tales of The Chosen. We have talked many heartbeats about both your people and mine, we have even laughed about how much the two are the same. But what the man said bothers me. We have always called ourselves The Chosen. But have your people always called themselves The Second People?"

"Yes we have."

"Are you sure? What about the tales that these people have? They sound a little different than the ones you have been telling." Ibex took her mate's hand and started walking slowly along the edge of the water. "They also use words and signs that are new to me and to you. They said that the words were from other bands further to the south and to the east. The new words help me to say what I am thinking even better than before. I like learning new words."

Gesher paused and smiled. "We taught each other many new words and signs when we first met. Your words were strange to me and my words were strange to you. It is good that there were many signs that we both knew. The words we both used were helpful in learning the new words and signs that you showed me."

Ibex leaned over and gently kissed her mate. "We have learned much from each other. Now as we travel we met new peoples and they show us things that are new, and use words that are new and different. It is good to learn new words and signs."

Bending over she picked up a stone that was almost perfectly round yet flat on the bottom. Bouncing it for a few heartbeats on her open palm she turned and shifted her grip slightly on the stone. Then she took the stone by the edge and threw it toward the water. The small stone hit the water, flew back into the air, hit the water again and again skipped back up off the water. On the fifth bounce it hit the water and it sank.

Gesher looked at the stone bouncing across the surface of the water. "What did you just do? Why did the stone not sink?"

Ibex squatted and picked up a handful of more stones. "We call it bouncing a stone. If you pick a stone that is almost round but has a flat side you can throw it and it bounces off the water. The young children like to do it. Usually when a boy or girl is grown and takes a mate they stop doing it. It is considered a child's game. Why I did it only the spirits know. But I saw the stone, picked it up and threw it."

"Show me how to hold it." Gesher said as he bent over and picked up a stone.

"Not that one," Ibex said glancing at the stone in her mate's hand. "It is not flat enough on the side that is the bottom."

"What side is the bottom? How do you know which side should be the bottom?"

Ibex shook her head and pointed at her stone. "The bottom is the side that is flat, or almost flat. It is the side that is close to the water. You throw it across the water keeping it as flat as possible. Do not aim high or low, just aim as if you were trying to hit something only a few steps in front of you. Balance the stone on

2

top of your long finger and grip it loosely between your thumb and the finger closest to the thumb."

Gesher threw the stone as hard as he could, as far as he could, and watched it hit the water and immediately sink. "It didn't bounce, what happened?"

Ibex couldn't believe Gesher. He was almost upset that the stone did not bounce off the water. "You threw it too hard and you should try hitting the water almost flat. It is almost the same as throwing your spear at something that is only a few steps away. Try imagining that it's a newborn deer that you found and it is not moving because it thinks you do not see it. Think of the stone as a spear and the water as a newborn animal that you found while hunting."

Gesher took another stone and balanced it on his hand. Muttering to himself he felt for the edges as his eyes stared at the surface of the water. "It can't be that hard."

Fawn stood there beside him for a heartbeat then picked up a stone and threw it gently yet firmly so it skimmed the surface of the water. It hit, then bounced up, went a short distance, hit the water again and ricocheted back into the air. The third bounce off the water was only a short distance and when it again hit the water it sank.

Gesher looked at Fawn and shook his head. "You can do it?"

"Of course I can Dada," she answered softly. "It is a game that all the children of The Chosen play. I saw one boy make a stone bounce on the water six times before the Spirit of The Water pulled it under."

Gesher sighed and again felt the edges of the stone. "Spirit of Gesher," he whispered very softly "Help me make the stone bounce off the water." His arm twisted as the stone hurtled out of his grasp. It hit the surface of the water and bounced back up. It traveled about the length of his arm and hit the water again and sank. Gesher smiled then yelled. "I did it, I made the stone bounce on the water. Did you see it?"

Fawn nodded and smiled. Her Dada was happy; it was one of the few heartbeats when she had actually seen him smile. He was a good Dada; he was a good provider and even a protector. But he was almost always very serious. He hardly ever laughed but then he never cried either. It was good to see him showing how happy he was. "Try again Dada."

Lynx walked up to his family gathered around the shore of the water. "What is everyone doing?"

"We are bouncing stones off the water."

Lynx shrugged his shoulders and began looking for a stone. His eyes seemed to glow as he spotted a stone that was almost perfectly round yet completely flat on one side. "Watch this," he shouted, as he pulled his arm back and with a twisting motion to his wrist and forearm threw the stone. It hit the water and bounced back into the air, went about three paces and hit the water bounced off and went another two paces before hitting the water for a third time. But then it rebounded again as it went about the distance of a man's foot before hitting the water and sinking. "Four bounces," Lynx yelled, "it went four bounces before sinking."

Gesher looked at his son. "How did you learn to do that?"

"Mama showed me the way to do it. She said that it was a game but that it also taught boys and girls how to use a stone to kill small animals and even nesting birds."

"When did she show you this secret? I never knew of it."

"I don't remember when, but I would also go with her with Fawn when Fawn was playing the game. If you said for me to stay with the females while you hunted, the three of us would play the game. Sometimes we would go hunting for birds or animals that were close to the cave. If you hit them in the head or body with a stone

4

there is no damage to the skin like there would be where a spear would have entered."

Ibex tugged on Gesher's arm. "Enough of this, we have to talk."

"In a few heartbeats," he answered picking up another stone. "I want to see if I can make the stone bounce at least three bounces before it sinks."

"Gesher, it is a child's game."

He turned toward her and the scowl on his face said more than many words could have. "It is not!" He said softly yet with a pent up anger in his voice that was easy to hear. "I think it could be a very good way to begin to teach hunting skills to children that are as young as three birthing seasons. Do you know what that could mean?"

"I don't care we – have – to – talk!"

"We will talk, I promise, but think of what this game as you call it could do. It can be a way for the youngest of the children to begin to learn how to use their eyes and hands together to do something. It is a way for them to begin to learn skills that they will need as they grow."

Ibex paused for a heartbeat as she thought of what he had said. But she wanted to talk and the ideas that he was talking about were not really understood. "Gesher," she said again and those around her could hear the pent up anger in her voice as she again said to her mate "WE – HAVE – TO – TALK."

"Alright, we will talk, but look at Fawn and Lynx throwing the stones so they bounce and hit then bounce and hit again and again on the water. See the other children coming and also picking up stones to throw. There is one trying to throw a stone and she is only learning to walk. I still say that this game is a great way to show the children how to use both their eyes and arms at the same heartbeat and to do something that teaches them how."

5

Ibex looked at Gesher and smiled. He was right. Why had no one in The Chosen thought of that? The idea of starting children as young as three, maybe even two, birthing seasons learning how to throw a stone could become a way to make learning other things a game.

"We have another game," she said as she took Gesher's arm. I will show it to you later. But now we have to talk. I need to learn as much as possible about the people you call The Second People, and I will tell you all I know about The Chosen."

"I have told you almost everything I know about my old people. The Second People are my old people. I am now Gesher of The Chosen."

"Yes, of course you are. But tell me again the story of how The Second People started. I want to hear it again, and then I will tell you the story of how The Chosen started. Our tales are almost the same I think." Ibex sat down under the massive limbs of an oak and leaned against it. "Even most of our beliefs are the same even if they are slightly different."

Gesher sat down beside her then lowered his head until it was in her lap. Closing his eyes he started to smile. There was something about having his head resting in her lap that was very relaxing.

"Mother," the shout brought both Gesher and Ibex to their feet. Gesher saw Fawn running toward them and she was sending hand signs as she ran. "It happened, it finally happened. Now Lynx and I can be called a mated couple. The Moon Spirit came! I am bleeding! It is the third time and that means that I am now a grown woman."

Ibex looked at Gesher and her smile was nearly as big as Fawn's. "She is right, now Lynx and Fawn can be mated. Now they can sleep together at their own hearth as a man and woman. It is the way of The Chosen."

"I am still a little bothered by calling the spirit who makes females bleed The Moon Spirit. I grew up hearing about The Spirit of All Women. This idea of a Moon Spirit that makes women bleed does not seem right. Men know of The Moon Spirit as much as they know of The Sun Spirit. Both men and women know of and honor both spirits."

"Gesher, how many times must I tell you? The Chosen honor The Moon Spirit, but the females of The Chosen give the spirit a special place in their hearts and in their ceremonies. The tales of The Chosen when this happens are well known. It is a sign that a woman will bleed every moon until she is expecting. Then The Moon Spirit does not come again until many days after the baby is born. In fact it usually is a moon or more."

"But," Gesher started to say but then stopped. "I guess that this is another reason why you said that we needed to talk. I think that I was not really paying attention to many of the stories and beliefs of The Chosen when you were telling them to me. I need to hear them again and this time I will not talk or think of other things."

Ibex looked at her mate and shook her head. He was a wonderful mate and certainly a caring man, but he did have a tendency to look right at her and yet ignore her.

The yells from back in the camp made them all turn their heads. One of the younger men was running toward them. "A large herd of bison was spotted. We are forming a hunting party to go and kill as many as we can. We hope to force them into a canyon so that they can't escape. Does anyone want to join us?"

Ibex looked at the young man and then at her mate and children. "Of course we do. But why are you chasing them into a canyon?"

The young male looked at Ibex. "If we force them into a canyon, we have a better chance of killing many before they escape. The sides of the canyon stop them from being able to bolt right or left."

7

Gesher nodded in agreement. "Of course we will join you. The more spears the better. Especially for big animals like bison. What direction are they?"

"North, toward the high peak."

Ibex's eyes grew large at the mention of a high peak. "This high peak, is it part of the canyon? How high is it?"

"No, it is further away. The canyon runs north and south and narrows quite a bit before it turns toward the river. The bison will turn before they reach the river. We have to get to them before they can get to the water."

"No we don't." Ibex shouted. "Why try to get them before they reach the river?"

"Because if they reach the river, they may swim across then turn and come back down toward the open valley on the other side. It is very dangerous over on the other side. There is a sharp cliff that is as high as 20 men are tall."

Ibex looked at Gesher and winked. "The spirits just sent us a lot of meat and skins."

Gesher nodded in agreement. He knew exactly what she was thinking. She had told him of the way The Chosen used cliffs to hunt. He closed his eyes and almost saw the animals hurtling over the edge of the precipice to their deaths. "It is a good sign."

Fawn and Lynx were also smiling and nodding their heads. Fawn grabbed Lynx's hand and started running toward the place were the hunting party was gathering. "It is a very good sign, the spirits have sent two signs to show that we are to be a mated pair. First The Moon Spirit came to me for the third time and now this herd of bison come all on the same day."

The young hunter stood there completely confused. What were they talking about?

Ibex saw his confused look and took him by the hand. "The Chosen have a way to hunt large animals that is not as dangerous as what you are used to doing. If there is a large cliff close to where the animals are, we use fire and loud noises to scare them into running off the cliff. Take me to your hunt leader and I will explain."

The large man stood there with his hands on his hips and glared at Ibex. "I don't care what your so called Chosen do, we are not going to try and chase the bison off a cliff just using fire and loud noises. It will not succeed. We have never done it that way and I will not be the first of The Second People to even consider it."

Gesher looked at the man and saw the look in his eyes. "I was unsure also," he said slowly sending a signal to the huge man who was the leader of the hunt. "But we, just the four of us, have used that very tactic many times while hunting. Once the four of us were able to scare seventeen horses into jumping off a cliff. We had enough skins and meat to last us for a full winter. It sounds strange, but it works."

"I am the hunt leader and I say no, it is not our way. The time to talk is over. Now you have to decide if you are going to join us in our hunt or stay here. If you come and join us, you will do as I say."

Fawn saw that her mother and father were not going to convince the hunt leader of the tactic that they had been using for many seasons. Seeing three young men standing close to her she motioned them closer. "You should try to convince your hunt leader to listen. Forcing animals to flee for their lives using fire and loud noise is safer than chasing them and using spears. All it takes is a few animals, hopefully the leaders, to panic and flee. When that happens the rest follow. Then as they get near the edge of the cliff the ones in the front try to stop or turn away from the cliff. But the ones in the back keep running forward and actually it is they who push the animals in front off the cliff. Then all we have to do is let the rest of the herd escape while we go to the bottom of the cliff and slaughter the few who are still alive. But even that is safe because most are so injured that they can not get to their feet."

The hunt leader saw Fawn talking to the three young men and strode over to where they were. "Do not listen to what they are saying. No one in this band will hunt that way."

The one young man, the one who had come and mentioned the hunt to the four strangers, looked at the man and shook his head. "Why not?"

"Why not?" The man almost screamed and for the briefest of heartbeats Gesher thought that the man was actually going to hit the boy. "Because I am the leader of the hunt and it is my responsibility, and only my responsibility, to make sure that the hunt is successful. If we fail, no one will be blamed except me. I will not allow this band to try something new that has never been done before."

"But," he started to say.

"If you want to chase animals off a cliff, then go with them." The big man shouted so loudly that all those in the camp stopped whatever they were doing and looked at him. "As long as I am in charge of this band's hunting, no one in this band will ever hunt any way other than the way we have always done it."

A young girl strode up to where they were talking, or actually now yelling. "I may be young, but I can remember many hunts where one or more of our hunters returned with injuries. I even know of two hunts where a hunter was killed. If we try - - "

Her head snapped back from the force of the blow and tears sprang into her eyes. For a heartbeat she stood there starring at the man then turned and raced away holding her cheek where his hand had hit her.

Ibex looked at Gesher and her eyes grew larger as she saw the girl running away. She flashed her mate a signal then turned and walked away. He saw the sign that she sent him and tapped Lynx on the shoulder then motioned to Fawn. "We are leaving, we will not stay in a camp, or with a band, were a man hits a young girl."

Lynx nodded and without even realizing what he was doing, or even that he had done it, placed his arm around the waist of Fawn. "Gesher is right!" He said with just enough force in his voice to make her glance up at him. "No male should ever strike a female like he did." He stopped and looked back toward where the young girl had run but he could not see her. "All she did was say what she was thinking."

Fawn felt his arm on her waist and moved ever so slightly closer so that her leg was brushing his. "Talking is good, it is the way that we learn what the other is thinking. Sometimes the best ideas are learned by listening."

Lynx felt the gentle pressure of Fawn's leg as it brushed against his leg. He felt the urge rising as he pulled her even closer. Lowering his head so that his lips were just above her ear he whispered, "I have an idea."

Fawn lifted her head and her eyes found his. "I have an idea also, and now that The Moon Spirit has come three times, we are mates. Remember that secluded clearing in the middle of the small clump of pine?"

"I remember!" He whispered as he took in a deep breath.

"I bet I can beat you there," Fawn said as she slipped out of his grasp.

"Where are the two of you going?" Gesher shouted as he saw them race away. "We have to get ready to leave."

Ibex smiled and pulled on his arm. "They are young, and now that Fawn is a woman, they are ready to become a mated pair. They are going off to make love. Be patient, they will be back very soon."

11

"Oh!" Gesher said and then he smiled. "I still think of it as mating, but you call it making love."

"I told you why. I started calling it making love when I realized that I loved you. It took me a long time to understand what love is. I had never experienced that feeling before. My old mate, Bear and I mated, but I never enjoyed it like I do when we are together. That is why I call it making love."

"We have learned many new words and ways of doing things from each other. We have even traded skills, lore and words with the clans of The Chosen and the bands of The Second People. They now use our words and we use their words. It is good to learn new ways and words from other people."

"Yes, it is," Ibex said in agreement. "It helps us to survive."

2

Gesher stood on the edge of the outcropping and shielded his eyes from the glare of the sun. He had to look west and the setting sun was directly in his face. Lynx walked up beside him and tapped him on the shoulder. Wolf strode up on the other side of Gesher and all three men stared at the raging currents swirling between the high cliffs.

After a few heartbeats, Gesher turned and started back toward where the three females were waiting. Shaking his head, he muttered more to himself than the two men walking alongside him. "It has taken us three days to climb this far, and it will take three more to get back down to where we were."

Wolf fell into step along side Lynx and whispered softly. "He is very upset. I have never seen him acting that way."

Lynx slowed his pace just a little to allow Gesher to widen the gap between them. "He gets that way when he is worried. It has been nearly 12 moons since we left your camp and continued our trek toward the east. Now we have two women who are expecting with your mate Rabbit, due to have her baby any day. My mate Fawn is also nearly due, she should have the baby in another moon. Gesher is very aware of the coming births and is worried about finding a safe secure place for all of us before the babies are born."

Wolf shook his head, and then just shrugged. "I am glad that Rabbit and I left our band to join with you. Since we started this journey with you I have learned many new things. This woman, Ibex may be different than I am; she and your mate Fawn certainly look different, but she is very knowledgeable and wise in the ways of the animals."

"She and Fawn are of The Chosen, I am also of The Chosen even if my Dada, Gesher, is not. You have to remember that now that you are one of this clan you are one of The Chosen. Ibex says that there is a small clan of The Chosen in the valley on the other side of this mountain. That is why we are trying to find a way to cross the peaks and then go to the other side into the valley. It will be good to find some people again so that we can trade stories, tools and other goods." Lynx pointed down the trail and then shouted to his mate. "There is no way across the river up here. We will have to backtrack and try another trail."

"Not today!" Fawn shouted back "Rabbit has started to have the baby. Ibex took her over to that patch of grass we passed about ten spears throws ago."

"The baby is coming?" Wolf screamed and rushed past Lynx and then past Gesher as he raced down the trail.

Gesher looked at Ibex and smiled. "Soon the Clan of Ibex will number seven. Then after another moon, or perhaps a little longer, it will be up to eight."

Ibex knelt next to Rabbit and felt her belly. "Yes, the baby is definitely coming. I can feel it moving lower. We have to get ready."

Gesher saw Wolf moving into position in front of Rabbit. "Watch what he is doing," He whispered to Lynx. "It is something that you will be doing when Fawn starts to have her baby. It is important for the man to be there for the female and let her use him to help her stay in position as the baby is born."

Fawn sat next to her friend and held her hand. "You can squeeze my hand if you want."

Rabbit glanced up and grinned at her traveling companion and friend. "Don't worry, I will."

14

Lynx saw the worry on his father's face and tapped him on the shoulder. "What is the matter? I can see on your face that something is bothering you."

"The baby is coming, and soon another baby will be here. Ibex says that there is a clan living just beyond these mountains. If a clan lives here, why is there no sign? I have not seen any footprints, no indication of fire, no hints of people anywhere."

"We have traveled many moons without ever seeing other people. From the time we found Fawn as a little baby, until she was almost a woman, we never found another group of people."

"You are right, but we were looking. Without finding other people we will not be able to trade. We will not be able to learn new ways of doing things. It was by finding and visiting other bands that the ways of Anbessa were taught to other bands. Now as we saw, when we were with the people that Wolf and Rabbit were part of, the ways of Anbessa are well known."

"But," Lynx started to say but then stopped as he realized what Gesher had said. When they had found the band that was sick from the bad water, both groups had benefited. His clan had grown by two individuals when Wolf and Rabbit had decided to leave their band and join their clan. They had been able to show the band the way of The Second People. The way to set up windbreaks and shelters within their caves. Then they were shown the new way to make spear points that would keep fish from slipping off the tip of the spear.

"You're right," Lynx mentioned to Gesher. "Meeting other groups of people lets us learn from each other. I like this new spear point for fishing. The little barb on the end of the point, the one pointing backward toward the shaft, keeps the fish from slipping off."

"They benefited from our skills also." Gesher said as he walked with his son toward the tallest pine and motioned for him to sit. "I think they were very happy to learn of the windbreak for the mouth of their cave and the shelters for deep inside the cave. Now they will have more protection from the cold winds blowing out of the north during the long cold winter."

Lynx sat next to the man he called Dada and shook his head. "I do know that they were surprised at the many new words and signs that we use. I did not know that the words and expressions along with the signs and signals we use could be so strange to others."

Gesher nodded slowly, "we use many words and signs from The Chosen that these people have never seen or heard. Your mother has shown us many ways of saying things we never knew or had words or signs for. When we meet a clan from The Chosen, they will also be hearing words and seeing signs that they do not know; words and signs from The Second People that I taught to Ibex. You and Fawn grew up knowing and using both the words and signs of The Second People and the words and signs of The Chosen."

Lynx shrugged his shoulders and smiled. "I guess," he said slowly, "that we are the first to use words and signs from both The Second People and The Chosen."

Lynx rose to his feet and began to walk back toward the comforting fire that burned next to where Rabbit and Fawn, along with Wolf and Ibex, were. "I am going to see what is happening, perhaps it is time for her to give birth to the baby."

"I think I will go and see what is on the other side of that gap, the one that is almost hidden from view by the thick pines to the south. Perhaps there is a way through there to the valley where Ibex says a clan of The Chosen live."

"Not alone you won't." Lynx said. "The pines are so tall and close together that it is almost impossible to walk through them. Who will watch the back trail if you go alone?"

"I traveled alone for many birthing seasons before I found Ibex. I let the spirits watch my back trail."

"That is not good enough now," Lynx said as he grabbed three spears and a heavy club. "I will go with you and watch the back trail while you lead the way."

Fawn glanced up and saw her mate and her Dada picking up spears and clubs. "What is going on?"

"We are going to go look for that clan that Ibex said is around here." Lynx answered as he turned to follow Gesher. "If they are as close as Mama thinks, then we should see some sort of sign by the time we clear the gap."

Ibex glanced up at her mate and her son. "Be careful and watch your back trail. The Chosen are very wary and will stay hidden when strangers come to their valley. They will be aware of you before you are aware of them."

Gesher walked over to his mate and pulled her to her feet. His kiss was long and tender. "I will remember all that you have taught me about the people who call themselves The Chosen. I will also remember the words and signs that they will know that mean we are friends and want to trade."

Fawn pulled her hand free from the grasp of Rabbit and pulled her mate's head toward her open lips. "I want to feel your lips on mine and your tongue flicking the top of my mouth. Kiss me as if you were going to leave for a full moon."

A moan from Rabbit made Fawn and Ibex turn back toward the woman. Wolf bent his knees even more to let his mate use his shoulders to grip as she struggled to give birth.

Gesher paused for a heartbeat as he thought about going or if he and Lynx should stay. "Ibex," he said softly, "do you need me here to help with the birth?"

"No, go. I have plenty of Fenigreek to stimulate the birth if it is needed and also more than enough Verbena for her pain. But I do not want to use them if it is not needed. She is young and healthy so the birth should be easy. You and Lynx go and look for the clan."

Twisting his head to look at the two men, Wolf balanced on one hand while trying to send a signal to them. His mouth silently formed the words his one hand was having problems signing. "Go and find them. I will be here to watch and protect the baby when it is born. As soon as I cut the cord and wash it, I will stand guard until you return."

Ibex bent over Fawn's shoulder and watched her daughter help with the birth. "Good," she said quietly and patted Fawn on the shoulder, "you are doing what needs to be done." She glanced up as Gesher and Lynx entered the thick pines. "Wait," she yelled.

Gesher stepped back out of the shadows from the massive pines. "What is wrong?"

"I just remembered. We could use some fresh Nepeta and Carum if you see any. The supply of Horseheal and Heal all is getting low. Try to find some and bring it back, you know what parts of the plants we need."

"I will watch for any healing plants along our trail. If I can't find any while we are going, I will search just for them on the way back. I will leave a trail that is easy to follow if you have to come looking for us."

"You worry too much." Ibex muttered. "Now go!"

Gesher pushed his way through the heavy thick hanging branches of the thick pine forest. In some places it was so substantial that he had to get down on his hands and knees in order to see more than a few paces.

Behind him Lynx kept glancing back the way they had come and then back at his father. "Slow down a little," he whispered with just a hint of urgency in his voice. "I am having a hard time watching where you are going and where we have been." If I take my eyes off you for more than a heartbeat or two, you seem to disappear."

"I think I see a small clearing just a little ahead of me. We will rest there and try to think of what has to be done. I have been watching the sun as it moves across the sky; we are still going toward the gap. This forest is too thick and we could never travel through here to get to the gap. I have never seen a forest like this."

Lynx suddenly lunged toward his father and tapped him on the shoulder. "I smell something and it is a strange scent, it is familiar yet somewhat unknown, I do not know if it is one I have smelled before!"

Gesher stopped moving and opened his mouth. He inhaled slowly through his mouth and nose tasting the air with his moist tongue as he also inhaled through his nose trying to identify any scent on the air. He placed a hand in back of his one ear and bent it forward in order to hear any sound no matter how small. His eyes darted back and forth searching for anything that was not where it should be. Nothing! He could see absolutely nothing, smell nothing strange, hear a sound that was not natural. Everything seemed completely as it should be. But Lynx was the son of Ibex; if he had her ability to smell then he must have smelled something. But what had he smelled?"

Dropping to his belly, Gesher began moving back the way he had come. As he passed Lynx, he signaled carefully to his son as his mouth silently formed the words. "If you caught a scent, then we have to find out what it is. It may be nothing, but it could be anything. Maybe it is danger or maybe it is not, but to ignore it would not be good."

"I still smell it and it seems to be moving," Lynx signed and mouthed silently.

"Moving, like an animal moves?"

"Yes, it is definitely moving. When I first smelled it, the scent was almost right out of the north. Now it is coming from the east and the wind has not changed."

Gesher gripped one of his spears just a little tighter as he wiggled past Lynx. "What about sounds, have you heard anything?"

"Nothing, there is no sounds except the normal sounds of the bugs, animals and birds that we hear all the time." The signs and mouth said the words but no sound was heard.

"But you," Gesher started to sign when he saw a foot, a human foot, so close that he could have reached out and touched it.

Gesher just pointed toward the foot. Lynx saw where his father's finger was pointing and watched a foot slowly and carefully touch the ground. He saw the toe feel the ground for anything that could break or make any noise. Then the rest of the foot moved lower until the heel came in contact with the firm dirt that made up the ground. A heartbeat later the other foot began doing the same thing. First the toe searching for anything that would make a sound, then when it did not encounter anything, the rest of the foot followed just as slowly and just as carefully.

Inhaling slowly Gesher rolled over onto his back. Sending a signal to Lynx and then saying a silent prayer to his guardian spirit he opened his mouth. The words that he barely whispered were the ones that he and Ibex had gone over many times as they talked about what to say when the first people from The Chosen were seen. "I am called Gesher from the Clan of Ibex. We are here to seek friends and to trade."

"Why do you crawl on your belly like a snake?"

"To see further than I can see if I stand."

"Only snakes, worms and those things that want to stay unseen crawl on the ground. Do you want to be unseen or are you a snake? Or are you a worm?"

Lynx heard the words and felt his anger rising in his heart. For anyone to be called a snake was one of the worst insults anyone could be called. But to be called a worm was even worse. Worms were the ones that crawled through the dirt not on top like a snake.

"I am a man who wants to trade and to make you a friend," Gesher answered slowly as he rose off the ground and tried to stand upright in the tangle of pine branches.

"What of the other one?" The voice asked quietly, "is he a man or is he a snake or perhaps a worm?"

"Lynx," Gesher almost shouted to his son, "stand and show yourself as a man."

"He is called Lynx?" The man standing in front of Gesher asked. "Lynx is a good name, it is one that The Chosen revere. I am also called Lynx. I am Lynx from the Clan of Baranja. But if he is Lynx who are you?"

Gesher pushed the heavy thick branches to the side and saw the man standing there. He raised his hand and signed the words as he spoke them. "I am Gesher from the Clan of Ibex. I, and my son Lynx, have traveled here to find you and to trade with you."

The man looked at Gesher and took a step backward. His spear suddenly was poised at the belly of Gesher in the stabbing position. "You talk like one of The Chosen but you look like a spirit. Have you come to take me to be with the spirits?"

Gesher paused for a few heartbeats before answering the man. He had not thought about how others may react to the color of his skin. Even Ibex who usually thought about everything well in advance had not anticipated such a question.

"I am not a spirit, I breathe as you do, my heart beats as your does. If I am hurt I feel pain, and if I am cut I bleed as you do. I am a man not a spirit."

21

"No man that I have ever seen looks as you do." The man held his spear poised and almost touching the belly of Gesher. "How can you be a man?"

"I am Gesher of the Clan of Ibex, a man of The Chosen, and a healer sent by my leader Ibex to find the clan who lives in these valleys. We are looking to trade spears, flints, hunting lore and other goods." Gesher motioned for Lynx to come closer. "This man is called Lynx, he is my son and the son of my mate Ibex."

"You are the mate of your leader?" But you are a man and leaders of clans are also men. How can your mate be the leader?"

"Our clan does have a female as a leader. She has been the leader from before Lynx was born. She, Ibex, is wise in the ways of The Chosen."

"The Chosen do not have females as leaders."

"I know of one clan that has a woman as a leader." Gesher answered slowly as he drew in a large breath.

"What clan?"

"Our clan."

"I have not known of the Clan of Ibex before this meeting. What valley do you call home? Where do you come from? How many people are in the Clan of Ibex?"

Gesher smiled at the man and held out his hand as Ibex had made sure to tell him was a good sign and definitely a signal of friendship. "My hand has no weapon as you can see. It is shown to you palm up as a sign of friendship."

"You know the signs and the signals of The Chosen, you talk like one of The Chosen, but you use words that I do not know. What are the words you are saying?"

22

Gesher looked at Lynx, the Lynx that was his son, and almost laughed. "It is the way we, the members of the Clan of Ibex, talk. We use words and signs from both The Chosen and The Second People. The Clan of Ibex is the first to combine both peoples' words, signs and signals. It is what our leader, Ibex, says helps us to know the ways of both The Chosen and The Second People."

The man from The Chosen who called himself Lynx looked at Gesher with a stare that seemed to be trying to see into his very spirit. "I want to hear more about this clan. Where do you come from? Why did you leave your valley? Why do you not answer my questions?"

"The valley we come from is far from here. We have traveled for many birthing seasons; I think you call it the time of new growth, or you may call it spring, to get to this mountain. Ibex and I started traveling when my son Lynx was still a toddler, now he is a man with a mate and soon his mate will have a baby. Why did we leave our valley? We left to find friends and to trade. It is important for people to go to new places to find new peoples and learn from others."

"Trade is good, friends are good. Having another clan help on a big hunt is good. But who are these Second People?"

"I used to be a member of The Second People before I became a member of the Clan of Ibex. The Second People live to the south of here. But they are following the edge of the great salt water and traveling up the rivers and streams into the valleys. We found a band of them not far from here. Many of them were sick from drinking bad water. Ibex who is a medicine woman treated them for their sickness and made most of them better. Three people did die from drinking the bad water."

"They are coming here into our valley?"

"If not this moon, then perhaps the next moon or the one after that. They like to travel and find new places to live. It is the way that

23

The Second People hunt and live. They stay in one place until the animals begin to fear them and then they move on."

"Do they all look like you?"

Gesher started to say yes when he realized what the man was trying to say. "No, I am different. The spirits made me to look like this to test me." He had wanted to say it differently but he realized that The Chosen would not understand some of the words he was trying to use. "My skin is the color of mother's milk and you can see the blood flowing under my skin. My hair and my eyes have no color. I am just one of only two that look like this. The only other one was the man who was the mate of my mother. He is now living with the spirits."

"What do the other people in your clan look like?"

"Take a good look at Lynx, he is the son of my mate Ibex. He has the look of Ibex but some say he also looks a little like I look."

"He looks thin, does he not eat enough?"

"He eats more than I do," Gesher laughed. Then reached in his traveling pack and pulled out a large hunk of meat. "He could eat all of this in one meal. But I would like to share it with you."

The massive man glanced at the piece of meat, then at Gesher and then at Lynx. "Come and meet my clan. We will eat and trade stories. I want my people to hear more about these ones you call The Second People. And," he added, looking Gesher straight in the eye, "I want them to see you. If they do not see you they will not believe me when I tell them about you."

Gesher nodded as he sent a signal to Lynx. "They must see me to believe I live."

"When they see you they will believe!" Lynx signaled back.

"Where are your people, where is the home of your clan?"

"In the valley where the water falls over the edge of the rock."

Gesher nodded his head up and down. "By a waterfall?"

The man stopped walking and looked back at Gesher. "Yes, by the high waterfall."

"Yes, it is!" The man said again as he turned and took to the trail. "We have been camping next to the pool under the waterfall. It is very cold and has a taste and smell that no other water has."

"So that is why we are following the water?"

"Walking in the water is not as hard as walking through the trees. The trees here are very old and grow very close together. We were following the stream to get to the hunting ground when we smelled you. It was a smell that we did not know and we came to find out what strange animal or bird had a scent like that. We did not know that the smell was from men. Do all of The Second People smell like you do?"

"Perhaps," Gesher said slowly as he increased his pace. "We just smell a little different from what you smell like."

"There," the man motioned and pointed downward, "is where our clan is camped. There is a ledge that twists many directions as it goes from up here where we are down to where they are. The trail is narrow in many places and has limbs from big trees hanging down almost covering the place where we will walk. We will have to be watchful where we put our feet so that we do not step on a stone and dislodge it. A stone kicked loose from up here can fall and hurt people below."

"We will be watchful as we walk."

"Wolverine," the man signed to the other hunter, "you go first and tell them that we found two strangers and are bringing them back for a meal. Be sure to tell them that one of them is very strange and that the children may be afraid. Then say that they should not be afraid that he is a man who walks on two feet just as they do. He is not a spirit come to take them away."

As Gesher, his son Lynx and the other man also called Lynx, descended the twisting trail that snaked downward from the top of the waterfall to the valley below, he started to tell the man of The Chosen about The Second People.

"The Second People are taller than you and The Chosen. They are strong and can carry much meat, but they are not as strong as The Chosen. I have seen my mate pick up and carry a load of meat or wood for the fire that many men of The Second People would not be able to lift. The men of The Second People care for their mates and children. They protect them with their lives against the animals of the forest and open plains. The Chosen call their group of families a clan. The Second People usually call their group of families a band. However, some do call it a clan. A few call it a tribe."

Lynx held up his hand in the easily recognized signal that said stop. "This is good to hear, but any man that would not protect his mate, and the children of his mate, even at the loss of his own life, is not a man."

"Yes, that is the same in all bands and clans," Gesher said quietly. "A man must protect his mate and her children. But," he added as he sent many hand signs to the man called Lynx, "The men of The Second People also are ready to die to save any female from their band, and any baby or child of any female from harm. I would die to save any female or any child from any clan of The Chosen or band of The Second People."

"If you died to save someone who was not of your clan, who would protect and feed your mate and her children?"

"The other men of the group would. The clan, or band, is only strong as long as it thinks as a group. Each person must think of what is best for the clan, and the clan must think of what is good

26

for each person. It is like the fingers on your two hands. You have two hands and ten fingers. Without the fingers, the hands cannot pick up anything. Each hand needs the five fingers, and the five fingers need the hand."

The slap on his back nearly sent Gesher falling off the edge of the trail. "It is good to hear that! The Chosen think the same. Every man, woman and child is important. Children are the gift of the spirits. A clan that has no children will soon be a clan that cannot feed or protect itself. Without children the clan will be no more."

Gesher looked at his son Lynx and winked. With his back turned toward the man of The Chosen named Lynx he silently mouthed, "that is what Ibex also says. I wanted to hear this man say the same words. It is good to hear him say it."

"Some are coming to meet us," Lynx said as he saw three men climbing up the curling-winding trail that ran from the valley up to the top of the ridge. "I think that they are very interested in seeing what a man looks like that has no color to his skin and whose hair is as white as the snow that is on the top of the mountains in winter."

Lynx reached over and touched his father on the shoulder. "Perhaps we should ask if they would send someone to our encampment and bring the others here?"

"What others?" The one from The Chosen named Lynx asked. "Are there other men with you?"

"One man is still back at the camp along with the three females that are our mates."

"You left your mates back at a camp? Why do you leave your mates to travel here?"

"As I have said," Gesher answered quietly, "we came to seek new friends and to trade. We have a new way to make a spear point so that you can spear fish while they swim in the streams and rivers."

"We do not like to eat fish, we are men. We eat meat from the animals that we kill. We eat fish only if there is not enough animals to kill so we can feed our families."

Gesher nodded his head slowly up and down. "I hear what you say and I agree, but fish can help get the hunger out of your bellies when the hunters return without fresh meat."

Lynx looked at Gesher and shook his head from side to side. "Our hunters are skilled in the ways of the animals we hunt. We have lived in this valley from the time of my mother's mother's mother's birth. Before that I think we also lived here but we have no tales to tell us."

"That is what Ibex has said. She is very knowledgeable in the lore and tales of The Chosen. I have been told that The Chosen have lived here for more birthing seasons, The Chosen call them springs, than be counted."

"That may be," the one from The Chosen who was called Lynx said. "Perhaps our medicine woman or one of the most revered and honored elders can tell you and remind me of more."

"I would like to hear more and to learn more, but I would like to have the rest of our clan brought here. My son Lynx can go with one or two men from your clan to our camp and bring the other members of our clan here."

"Yes, it is a good thought. Your son Lynx can go with Wolverine. Your Lynx can find your camp, and your people. Wolverine can follow the trail back here to our clan's home. It is a good plan."

3

Ibex pushed a large branch out of her view and smiled. There was the encampment of the clan. It looked exactly like she had thought it would look. It was definitely a camp of The Chosen. She saw so much that reminded her of her old camp; the one she had grown up in, the one she had become the mate of Bear in It brought back so many memories that she almost began to cry.

"We are here," Wolverine shouted. "Lynx and I have come back with the missing man, the three females and the new born baby. It is a male baby."

Gesher looked up from where he was sitting and saw the tiny infant wrapped in a large skin that his mother, Rabbit, was carrying him in. All that he could see was a small face peering out him. But the baby had eyes that seemed to be looking right at him, and they were so blue that he almost thought that he was imagining the color. "Here are the rest of the Clan of Ibex," he said as he rose to a standing position next to the old man of The Chosen, the one the rest reverently referred to as The Wise One.

The old man stood there with a younger man on either side of him helping him to maintain his posture. His hands shook as he sent a sign of welcome to the people approaching the encampment. "Welcome to the Clan of Vultur. Come sit and eat with us, share our fire."

Ibex extended her two hands and clasped his in hers. "I am Ibex, leader of the Clan of Ibex, and I am thankful for the welcome you have offered. We have traveled far, for many, many springs to come here."

"It is said that you come to trade and to meet new friends," the old man wheezed and then was racked by a violent series of coughing. "You have already found friends, but what do you have to trade?"

Ibex squatted on the ground and opened her traveling packs. "We have spear points that are made a new way. They have a barb that points backward toward the shaft of the spear. When you spear something it can not slip off."

"Gesher told me of that spear point," Lynx said, "The Chosen do not like to eat fish. We prefer the taste of bison, elk, horse and the other large animals that live here."

"Of course we don't," Ibex answered. "The Chosen are eaters of meat. But have you ever had a rabbit, or a hare, or a bird that you speared slip off your spear and get away? I have, and I know that the animal or bird will die from the wound. But even though I searched for it I could not follow the trail. The new spear point will keep small animals from getting away."

"Ahh," was all the man known as The Wise One said as he motioned the two young men holding him up to lower him to the ground.

Gesher looked at Ibex and the smile that spread across his face was a pale imitation of the thoughts that were flowing through his head. No wonder that I love her he thought without daring to say the words out loud. He knew that when the leaders of two clans were talking about trade or other things of importance, no one should speak, and no one should do anything to interrupt the talk. Why didn't I think of saying the spear point would work with small animals? She is thinking of the right things to say while I am still worrying about what has been said by the other people.

The Wise One sent a sign to Ibex to sit. "I have trouble talking," he signed to her. "Would you please just use hand signs?"

"Hand signs were used from the time the first people were pulled from the ground and made into people that could talk and think," she signed back. "Many children are using signs before they can even say their first word."

"That is true," he signed back and smiled at her. "You know the tales of The Chosen."

"I grew up hearing the stories and tales of our people. My mother was the medicine woman of our clan and also the teller of the legends." She signed using fluid motions.

"The teller of the legends is one to be revered," he signaled and just a faint glimmer of a smile tried to form on his face. "To also be the medicine woman of the clan is a special honor. To be both is a rare honor; your mother must have been regarded as a very special woman. "

"As you are!" Ibex replied almost a little too quickly. "I have heard about you from the man called Wolverine." This time she used both spoken words and her easily recognizable hand signs that seemed to move as if they had a mind of their own. "He told me of your skill and knowledge."

"I am but a shell of what I was," he signaled and his hands did not move as quickly or as easily as Ibex's hands. "When I was younger," then he stopped and this time a grin did split his face as he shook his head up and down. "You are indeed a wise leader. For just a few heartbeats I forgot what we are here to talk about."

"I am here to talk about anything you wish to talk about." Ibex signaled returning his grin. "We, my clan and I, are your guests. It is you who decides what we are going to talk about or even if we are going to talk. What do you want to say?"

"Tell me," he signed, "about this new spear point. Can I see one?"

Turning to Gesher, Ibex signaled silently. "Take two points that are not attached to shafts and give them to The Wise One."

31

Gesher nodded and reached into his large traveling pack. Picking out two of the best ones he gently placed them in the old man's trembling hand. "I made both of these myself," he signed. "They are made of the best flint I could find."

The Wise One nodded and motioned to one of the young men that seemed to be just a large step away regardless of where he was slowly meandering around the glowing fire. "What do you think?"

The man reached over and took the two pieces of flint that had been worked to a polished piece of perfection by Gesher. "Umm," he muttered then slapped a hand over his mouth as he realized that he made a sound.

"Speak," The Wise One said.

"It is a strange point, but as I look at it," he paused for a few heartbeats as he turned it over and over in his hands. "The barb, as they called it, should keep any small animal from slipping off the spear after it is speared." He turned it over a few more times as his fingers felt the edges and the sides of the point. "It could also be used on larger animals to keep the spear from being knocked out as the bison or deer runs. The blood trail would be smaller but the spear bouncing in the open wound as the animal runs should make the entry larger and cause more bleeding."

"So," The Wise One said with a little more strength to his voice, "what do you say?"

"It is good! We can use this new spear point; it is a good trade."

"What can we give in return?" The Wise One again started to sign his words.

"We have many skins."

Ibex shook her head from side to side. "We do not need skins."

"We have much meat to share."

Again Ibex shook her head from side to side. "We can give you meat."

"What do you want?" The Wise One signaled. "What does your clan need?"

"That is a question that needs much thought," Ibex signaled. "Why not eat and celebrate our new friendship while I talk to my clan about what we need?"

"Eating is good," he signed, "but you are the leader of your clan, do you not speak for all of them?"

"I am the leader," Ibex signed back, "but in the Clan of Ibex I seek ideas from those people who wish to talk. I have been taught about seeking opinions by my mate Gesher."

"That is a strange way of being a leader."

"It may be strange to your clan, but it is the way of the Clan of Ibex. It is the way we have done it since the time we were just two people. Many ideas have been said while we have talked and many times I have listened and heeded those words."

"It is strange," The Wise One again motioned as he signed for help in getting to his feet. "Not only have you shown us a new way to make a spear point, but you have given me a way to learn from my people. Perhaps, maybe, I will seek opinions from a few of my elders when I have to make a decision."

"I am sure that you will be given good council by those whose opinion you seek." Ibex signed as she also rose to her feet. "I will talk to Gesher and the others in my clan about what we would want in trade."

"Talk," The Wise One signed as he was helped to the fire where the meat was roasting. "We have much time before the night grows dark. You and your clan will spend the night with us?"

33

Ibex nodded her head up and down. "Of course we will stay for the night. It is good of you to offer."

"We brought meat to share," Wolf signed as he turned his traveling pack upside down and emptied it on the ground.

"We have much meat," the man called Lynx from The Chosen said, "we will share with the Clan of Ibex."

"We are the guests of your clan," Rabbit said quietly. "We would be honored to share with you."

"We will all share," Ibex said loudly as she signaled to her clan. We will share our meat and they will share their meat. It is good to share."

The Wise One looked at her out of the corner of his eye. I am the one who is called wise he thought silently, but she is the one who thought of a way to keep the members of both clans from getting upset over whose meat is shared. If I was not an old man, and if I did not already have a mate, I would ask her to join me as my mate and to add her people to mine. She is a wise woman who knows what to say when it is needed.

Gesher sat next to Fawn and patted her on her shoulder. "How are you feeling? Is the little one growing in your belly getting ready to be born?"

"I hope to the spirits that he is, or perhaps she is," Fawn answered as she tried to snuggle closer to him. "All I know is that I am more than ready. My belly is bigger than Rabbit's belly was when she had her baby."

"She is bigger than you, easily the width of my hand taller, so there is more room in her belly for the baby. A baby needs room, and the bigger the mother the more room in the belly, before the belly starts to push out."

"She may be taller but she can't do what I do." Fawn added as she grabbed at her belly. "I can carry more than she can. We were talking a few days before she gave birth and we decided that she is at least two springs older than I am. So she is older, she is taller, but I am stronger. And," Fawn added giving her Dada a wink, "she cannot smell the scents on the wind like I can."

"I can't either," Gesher sighed. "It seems that only you and Ibex have the ability to catch scents, and even tastes, that I can't. Sometimes Lynx can, but he is not as good as you or your mother. It seems that only those that are born into The Chosen have the keen noses." He looked over at his mate sitting next to The Wise One and smiled. "Those of us who choose to become a member of The Chosen do not have the ability to smell, or taste on the wind, what you do. You and the other people of The Chosen are special."

"Where is Lynx?" Fawn suddenly asked. "I do not see him."

Gesher turned his head and glanced around. "Somewhere, I guess, but I do not see him."

"Find him, get him now!" Fawn exclaimed as she grabbed her belly. "I need him now, the baby is coming."

"Now?" was all Gesher was able to say when Fawn grabbed his arm.

"Now!"

"Ibex," Gesher asked quietly as he sat next to her. "Have you seen where Lynx is?"

"No, I have no idea where he is. Why?"

"Fawn says that the baby is coming."

"Now?"

"Yes, now. That is why I want to find Lynx."

Ibex looked at her mate then she looked at The Wise One sitting next to her. "In the Clan of Ibex," she signed slowly, while speaking in a low voice so that he and those sitting close by could see her signs and also hear her words, "it is our custom to have the man help at the birth of the baby. One of our females is ready to have a baby so the male of her hearth is needed to help her have the baby."

"What are you saying?" The Wise One asked as he glanced at Ibex. "The males of The Chosen do not help at the birth. That is what females do, not males. No male wants to be near a female giving birth."

"The males of my clan do!" She answered quietly but with just enough force to make him look right at her. "It is our custom, we call it a tradition, and the mate of Fawn is needed now. Does anyone know where Lynx is?"

"I saw him and Lynx walking toward the bull rushes," one young female said. "They had said something about trying the new spear point on the large sturgeon that hides in the tall water grasses in the deep pool."

"Find him and tell him that he is needed now. That the time of birth is here."

The young girl leapt to her feet and ran toward the edge of the river. "I will find him," she yelled. "And I will bring him back."

The Wise One sent a flurry of hand signals to the two young men that were his constant companions. "Get me to a safe place, one away from the female that is having a baby. Then tell all of our men that it is time to find something to do that is away from here."

Both Ibex and Gesher saw the hand signals that were being sent and glanced at each other. "The meeting is over," Ibex said to Gesher as she rose to her feet. "I think that you should also go and look for Lynx, he may not realize the seriousness of the situation."

"Seriousness?" Gesher said as he looked at his mate. "Why would you say that Fawn having her baby now is serious?"

"We are in the campsite of another clan. A clan that does not believe in a male being near a female giving birth. When you in the home of another, you should follow their beliefs and customs."

"But," Gesher started to say when Ibex shook her head from side to side.

"But," she said softly, "we are going to follow our clan's customs and traditions. Lynx will help at the birth."

The yell from upstream made both of their head's turn. Gesher smiled at Ibex and she returned his smile. "I think," Gesher said as the yell was repeated, "that our son has gotten the message."

Lynx sat down next to his mate and took her hand in his. "The spirits are going to make you a Mama and me a Dada," he said as he leaned over and kissed her. "Soon we will know if we are going to have a baby girl or a baby boy."

"If it is a girl, will you be unhappy?" Fawn asked as another pain shot through her belly.

"Why would you ask that?" He said as he moved in front of her.

"You were born first, you are male. Men like a son first."

"Where did you hear that?"

"The women in the band that Rabbit and wolf came from told me."

"They are wrong!" Lynx said kissing his mate tenderly. "Remember that they are the same band where the hunt leader hit a young girl for just talking."

"I remember that, but does hitting someone make them wrong?"

37

"I would say that it does," Lynx answered softly. "Any band, or clan, that allows a man to hit a female must not respect what a woman is. If they do that, it is wrong, and if that is wrong, as we know it is, then how can anything they say be trusted?"

Fawn grimaced as another pain coursed through her belly. "But Wolf and Rabbit lived there."

"Wolf and Rabbit left that band of people and joined ours. They said they did not like the way that the hunt leader acted. It was Rabbit that he hit. She was just talking, saying what she thought and he hit her. Then, as she started to cry, it was Wolf who said he wanted to leave and he asked her to come with him."

"I remember," Fawn said. "Gesher told them that they were welcome to join our clan. He said that as long as they followed the customs of The Chosen, and forgot some of the ways of The Second People, they would be allowed to come and be members of our clan."

"They have been good members of our clan," Lynx whispered in her ear. "They have tried to forget everything about their old band. But what they still remember is good. Our clan is now a group of people from both The Second People and The Chosen. As Ibex said, we are now both. Did you not hear what she has been saying about us for many moons?"

"Yes," Fawn answered as she squatted and grabbed her mate's shoulders. "She said that we are blessed by the spirits because we have both peoples in our band."

Rabbit walked toward her mate with her baby suckling at her breast. "I guess that I never thought about being around a whole group of these people. Are you as nervous as I am being here? Some of these men are so big that I wonder what would happen if they got upset with us?"

"I'm not and neither is Gesher or Lynx," Wolf said as he put his arm around her.

"Well, I am." She replied as she pushed his arm away. "As a new father you should be concerned about your baby. Suppose that they have some ceremony, or perhaps a custom where they sacrifice babies to some spirit or another? Have you thought about that?"

"Why worry about things that Ibex and Gesher are not worried about? Ibex is the same as these people. If there was something to be worried about I think that she would have warned us."

"But," Rabbit said calmly yet her mate could sense the uneasiness in her voice. "Why are all the males picking up their spears and leaving?"

Wolf's head swiveled around and an involuntary gasp escaped his mouth. All the males, at least those that were adults along with those that were almost men, had formed a small group and were hurrying away. The only males that were still there were the young boys. Even the elder males and The Wise One were going. "You're right," he whispered as his gaze swept back and forth. "What is going on?"

"I told you," Rabbit almost screamed in his ear, "they are going away to plan their ceremony, or ritual, or something. Then they are coming back here and are going to sacrifice our baby. Maybe even kill all of us."

Gesher was walking close to where the two were arguing and turned toward where they were standing. "I heard what you said Rabbit and you are wrong. These people would not kill all of us and they certainly would not sacrifice your baby. They revere new life and honor all women who are mothers."

"Then where are the men going? Why are they leaving right now?"

"They are going hunting, or perhaps just taking the young men out for training on following a track."

"Why?" Rabbit asked as she continued to clasp her baby tightly to her.

Gesher smiled as he remembered what Ibex had told him when she realized that she was expecting. His smile spread even further as he thought of the reasons that Ibex called it expecting instead of being with child. "Listen to what Ibex told me," he said quietly as he gently pushed them a little farther away from where they were standing out toward the edge of the camp. "Men of The Chosen do not help with the birth. They look for something to do when it is time for the baby to be born. Ibex was terrified to find she was expecting and that there were no other females to help with the birth. When I told I could help she did not believe me. She said that men did not stay where a female was giving birth."

Gesher stopped walking and sat down on the grass. "Come and sit with me," he said to them and patted the ground next to where he was sitting. "Ibex told me that when a female realizes that she is going to have a baby, all the other women who have had babies come and talk to her. They tell her what to expect as her belly grows, what to expect after the baby is born, what to expect as the pains come. They even tell her what to expect her mate to say and do. That is why The Chosen call it expecting and not being with child. I think it is better to say that the woman is expecting."

"Yes, that I do know." Rabbit said just relaxing her grip on her baby a little. "We were calling it expecting whenever we talked. But why do the males leave? Our men stay and help."

"That is something only the spirits know," Gesher replied. "But they do leave. After the cries of the newborn are heard, they will return. They really have not gone that far. They would not leave the camp and the females unprotected."

"I thought so," Wolf said and smiled at his mate.

"No you didn't," was the quick reply. "If you knew, then why didn't you say so?"

"But," Wolf started to say but saw the look in her eyes and stopped. "You know better don't you? I was unsure myself, but now that Gesher has explained it to us, it does make sense. Not all peoples will do the same thing all the time. Some are different."

Gesher put his arm around the waist of Rabbit. "You are as safe here in this camp of The Chosen as you would be in our camp." Squeezing her waist just enough he whispered softly, "Maybe even safer than in the arms of Wolf." Then he laughed.

Wolf looked at Gesher with a look of puzzlement on his face. What had Gesher whispered to Rabbit? Why did he suddenly laugh? He was just about to ask when everyone in the camp heard the cry from Lynx. "The baby is coming, I can see the head!"

Gesher's arm slipped off Rabbit's waist and he started toward the center of the camp where Fawn and Lynx were. He had only taken a few steps when Ibex caught up to him. He paused to give her a kiss and then took her hand in his. "Another baby, another member of the Clan of Ibex, is it going to be a boy or a girl?"

"The spirits know, and soon we will." Ibex replied as she squatted next to Lynx and Fawn. "Gently, be gentle with the head, do not pull. Let the baby come out when it wants to. The spirits and the baby will decide when the birth will be."

Lynx glanced up from where he was sitting and saw the people gathering around him. Gesher was there as was Ibex and Wolf and Rabbit. But there were also many females of The Chosen, members of the Clan of Vultur standing there. But off in the distance, trying to stay hidden behind a large oak tree was a young man. The man was peering out as if trying to see what was happening but afraid to show himself or let people know he was there. He would look for a heartbeat or two, then disappear back behind the thick moss covered trunk. A few heartbeats later his head again could be seen as he tried to see what was happening.

41

Ibex glanced up at the females gathering around the place where Fawn was struggling to give birth. "This is the first baby that my daughter has had. The baby will be the first of my children's children. The spirits have been kind to me and let me live many springs so that I could see this."

One old woman pushed closer. Her hair, what there was of it was as white as snow and when she opened her mouth to talk Ibex saw that there were no teeth left in her mouth. "It is good to see the children of your children born." She wheezed as she tried to catch her breath then continued. "Three moons ago I saw the birth of a baby that was the first of my daughter's daughter."

Ibex looked closer at the old woman. "You are indeed honored by the spirits. To live to see the children of your children start to have babies must mean that you are special in the eyes of the spirits."

"If living so long that you need to have your food chewed for you like a baby, then I must be special. If living so long that your eyes can no longer see the leaves on the trees or the faces of children, then I am special." She coughed trying to catch her breath and wheezed many times. "If needing help just to move from your campfire to your sleeping place is being special, then I definitely am special."

"But," Gesher said as he tapped her on the shoulder to get her attention. "The spirits have blessed you with many things. How many children have you had?"

The question seemed to make the old woman stop and think. She closed her eyes and gently rubbed her chin. As she stood there, Gesher thought he could see the very start of tears trying to form in her eyes. A few heartbeats later she was crying.

"I gave birth to three children that lived beyond their birthing year. Two others died before they were weaned. My two sons have gone to be with the spirits. One died before he was ten springs old. The other died on his first hunt when a buffalo gored him. My daughter has also gone to join her siblings. She died five springs ago. My daughter had three children, two boys and a girl. The two boys are both with the spirits, but her daughter lives and it is she who had a baby three moons ago."

Wolf signaled silently to Rabbit. Then mouthed the words. "Three children born to her who lived more than one spring, and all three now with the spirits. The daughter had three babies and the baby of her daughter's daughter was born three moons ago."

"Yes, I did hear what she was saying. Three children, then the only one that lives has three babies. Then the baby was born three moons ago, it is strange." Rabbit mouthed silently as her hands sent back the message.

"It's a boy," Lynx almost shouted as he helped the baby onto the furs that his mate was squatting on. "Another boy for the Clan of Ibex."

The young man peaking out from behind the oak tree almost moved into full view. The motion was not completely missed by those gathered around Rabbit and Lynx. "We have someone very interested in what is happening," Wolf signaled to Gesher as he silently mouthed the words. "Look over by the large oak tree, the one with the moss almost covering the whole trunk. Someone, and it is a male, is watching the birth."

Gesher slowly walked a few paces then turned toward the oak. He studied it carefully then walked just one step toward the baby now crying on the soft skin. Mouthing his words silently he signaled to Wolf and Ibex. "There is definitely a young man trying to hide behind the oak and yet very interested in what is happening here. What do you think we should do?"

Wolf walked over to where Gesher was standing but kept glancing toward the oak. "Yes," he said softly as he got closer to where Gesher was. "He is definitely watching what is happening. Do you think we would scare him into fleeing if we signaled to him?"

"Perhaps, or maybe not." Gesher whispered. "Why don't you sneak around that way? Pretend that you are looking for something. I will go the other way and then we will both turn toward him. Count 100 paces then turn."

Wolf nodded and began to walk away from where Gesher was. As he walked he was counting quietly to himself. His pace seemed to increase slightly as he reached 90, then 91. At 99 he was walking quite rapidly and as he muttered 100 he spun around and shouted. "What are you looking at?"

Gesher had also reached 100 and he was moving toward the young man. As Wolf shouted, Gesher also added his voice to the question. "You do not have to hide behind a tree. You are welcome to come over by the fire and hold the baby. Why are you trying to hide from us?"

The young man seemed to be trying to slip into the very ground. He dropped down onto his hands and knees then his belly as he tried to slink away. He had been discovered. Why had he tried to see the birth of the baby he didn't know? But something, some inner voice or perhaps it was a spirit talking to him, made him move even closer. When the rest of the males in the clan had gone off to the very edge of the camp, he had managed to keep away from them. Now he had been discovered. What would the other men say, or even do?

"There is no need to try to flee," Wolf called out. "Come and see the newborn baby. I am sure that Lynx will let you hold him. The feel of the newborn snuggling into your arms is a feeling you will never forget."

Gesher moved to intercept the man, or actually young male on the verge of becoming a man. "We will not harm you, if that is what is worrying you. In the Clan of Ibex, watching and helping a woman give birth is one of our traditions. It is to be expected!"

Lynx stood up and watched the two men of his clan moving toward the boy who was not yet a man. "He is scared," he said to Fawn.

"He is showing signs of panic. A man, woman or even child who is panicked will do things that are unexpected."

Fawn nodded as she rose to her feet to see what was happening. "We have all seen how a panicked animal acts when it is pursued and then cornered. When it realizes that all hope of escape is gone, it can even attack the one chasing it. The deer will turn and fight the wolf; the hare will attack the wolf. It is the last desperate attempt to survive."

"And," Lynx said as he started toward the place where Wolf and Gesher had the young man cornered, "the youngster is cornered just like a prey animal by the predator."

"Give me our son," Fawn said as she kissed Lynx, "then try to help the young man. I can see his fear."

Nodding his head up and down, Lynx handed the baby to his mate. "Hold him to your breast and keep him warm. I will try to move closer. Why don't you just sit and talk to the baby? Perhaps, just perhaps, it will help."

"How?" Fawn asked as she lowered herself onto the ground.

"Only the spirits know, but the gentle sound of a mother's voice is always calming."

Ibex tapped Fawn on the shoulder. "Let's try talking in a voice that mimics the sounds of birds. Sometimes the sounds of birds calling to each other is a good way to signal. I think that making a whistling sound will help. You know the whistling sound for danger?"

"Of course I do," Fawn said and formed her lips into a pucker and began to whistle. The sound slowly built until it seemed to float across the meadow and into the edge of the trees. The sound reached both Wolf and Gesher. It sounded like a bird but both knew that it wasn't any bird making the sound. They had begun to use the whistling sound as a way to communicate with each other when the thick forests made hand signs impossible to see. The subtle differences between the sound that they heard and the real sounds of the bird were minimal, barely noticeable as they saw by the members of the clan gathered around them No one except their clan seemed to notice the insignificant yet very important changes in the song.

Gesher stopped pursuing the young man and sent a quick signal to Wolf. "Hold where you are, there may be a problem. Listen to the song signal."

"I hear it," Wolf responded and dropped to one knee. "It is Fawn, I can tell her whistle."

"So can I," Gesher flashed his reply. "Do you see any danger?"

"No, but I heard the sound of danger in her song. Fawn would not have sent a signal of danger unless she was worried. Did I also hear Ibex?"

"Yes, you did." Gesher whispered as his hands flew to send his message. "If both Ibex and Fawn are sending the signal of danger, I fear that there is something we have not seen, smelled or heard."

As they paused the young man bolted. He had seen the two men stop and smell the air. He had paused for the briefest of a heartbeat when he saw them tilt their heads upward and the way they inhaled. It was the position all people took when they wanted to, or were trying to, identify a scent on the air. He had inhaled briefly then when he could find no scent other than the ones that he was used too on the calm air, he had jumped to his feet and started to run. The only danger that he could identify was the two men from the Clan of Ibex who had been moving close to his hiding place.

In the distance he saw the other males from his clan returning. They had not been far, never more than a few spear throws from the camp, and had heard the sound of the baby as it took in its first breath. Now that the birthing had taken place they could return and again do what was needed in and around their hearths. Should he rush to them and seek their safety? Or should he turn and flee in another direction?

He was about to shout to them when he saw their leader point to him. He could not hear the words that were spoken but he saw the signs and even at the distance he was from them, was sure he could read the words on the old man's lips.

The whole group had paused and looked right at him. Then The Wise One had lifted his trembling hand and pointed right at him. The young man saw The Wise One pointing at him and dropped back onto the ground. "Spirits help me," he pleaded. "I was wrong and stayed back to try to see the birth of the baby. Now the men are coming back and The Wise One knows what I did."

Ibex saw the group of men returning and also the way the young man was acting. He was petrified! She changed the tone and pitch of her voice so that it sounded like an owl hooting in the dark of the night. But it was not night it was the bright glare of the sun. The sounds she made caused all the members of her clan to stop and look right at her. Her hands flew as she mouthed the words.

"Move quickly and get between the returning men and the young man that was hiding behind the tree. I may be wrong but I fear that something bad is going to happen."

The old woman who had told them that she had seen the birth of a baby to the daughter of her daughter sent a signal to Ibex. "You are right, he has broken one of our taboos. I saw him trying to peek from behind the oak but did not say anything. For a male to stay where a woman is birthing a baby is not acceptable. Our memories go back to the beginning when the spirits pulled the first of The Chosen from the ground. No male, at least an adult male, should be near a female who is birthing a baby. It is taboo!"

Ibex nodded in understanding as she began to run toward the place she had seen that was about one spear throw from the returning men and one spear throw from the trembling young man who was now sprawled on the ground. "I know of what you speak. When I found out I was expecting I tried to flee from Gesher. It was Gesher who told me that the males from his people not only stayed where a female was giving birth, but also helped with the birth. Gesher not only was there when Lynx was born, he held me and then cut the birthing cord that joins the mother to the baby."

"I saw how your males help. I was there when Wolf stayed with Rabbit as she birthed the baby. It was a sight I had never seen before. Now the spirits have shown me everything I need to ever see. If I had not seen it with my own eyes, and anyone had told me that it was done, I would not have believed it possible."

"The Clan of Ibex does not have that taboo. In our clan we want the males to be there and to help. The male, who we call the Dada, picks up the baby as soon as it is born and gives it the breath of life then cuts the cord."

The Wise One held up his trembling arm. "Did Fox stay and watch a female birthing a baby?" The question was not asked to get a response from the other males. The Wise One asked the question as a statement that he already knew the answer too.

Wolverine tapped The Wise One on the shoulder as he pointed toward the ground where Fox lay trembling. "Ibex and her clan are moving toward the place where Fox is on the ground. I think that they are trying to get between us and him."

Nodding his head up and down The Wise One sent a sign for the men to stop and sit. "Ibex," he then signed as he tried to yell to her but couldn't. "What are you doing?"

"I am trying to stop you and your clan from doing what I fear you are planning on doing."

"Fox did what no male should ever do. He is a male who will soon be named a man. He broke a taboo, a custom of The Chosen, and he will be punished."

Gesher put his arm around Ibex and then turned to face The Wise One and the rest of the men. "But as you say, he will soon be named a man, that means he is not yet a man." Gesher took a deep breath and then spoke loudly so all could hear his words and not misunderstand them. "A man knows the ways of his people, a boy is just learning them. Boys and young girls make mistakes, it is the way of youth. Would any people punish a youngster for doing what young people do?"

"He is old enough to know what is right and what is wrong." Wolverine shouted back as he took two steps toward where Ibex, Gesher, Lynx, Fawn and the rest of the Clan of Ibex had formed a line. "Babies and young children make mistakes that is true. But Fox is not a child. He is to be named a man of the clan at the next full moon, when the moon shows her full face and we can see her eyes, nose and mouth. He must be punished."

"Wolverine speaks what we all think," the other man called Lynx said. Fox must face the punishment. If we fail to do what is demanded, the clan may be punished by the spirits."

Ibex looked at Gesher and shook her head from side to side. "I know the punishment that they are talking about. Remember what I told you about being forced out of the clan to live alone. It is death waiting to happen. They are going to banish him."

Gesher nodded and then leaned over so that his mouth was just actually touching Ibex's ear. "When I found you, or we found each other, you talked about dying. You said that you were a woman without a clan. It took me a long time to understand what it was that you were saying about being alone. Do you think that they would really send Fox out alone, banish him, I think the word was exile, just for trying to see the birth of a baby?"

"The Chosen have lived for more springs than can be counted by following their customs and taboos. We should have talked about the taboos that The Chosen have. Now it is too late to talk about them. The taboos, or customs that they have – you and I call them traditions – are what make The Chosen, The Chosen. Without their lore, their beliefs, their oneness with the animals, birds and all living things that live side by side with them, The Chosen would not be The Chosen. You have wondered about my being able to smell scents that you can't, about my being able to follow a track where you see no sign. I can't explain it but it is as if I am the animal making the track. I become that animal as I hunt it."

Gesher nodded as if he understood, but he really did not. How could a hunter become the animal that is being hunted? "You continue to make me happy that I met you." Gesher said as he glared at Wolverine. "I think that I need to learn more about the lore and taboos of The Chosen as quickly as you can teach them to me."

"Fox," Wolverine shouted, "come here!"

The young man named Fox slowly rose to his feet. He glanced at the line of people standing between him and The Wise One along with the rest of the men from his clan. A shiver raced down his spine and he fought to keep the tears from his eyes. He knew what they wanted and what they were going to do.

Ibex turned her head as the sound of a twig snapping reached her ears. "He is coming this way," she whispered to those standing side by side with her. "But I want him to have to go around us, not through us. Do not let him go between anyone of us."

"Why?" Rabbit asked as she twisted around to see Fox walking toward them.

"The Chosen live by ritual and by symbolism. If we allow Fox to separate us, even if it is just to pass through to get to where The Wise One is, it will look as if we can be separated. That we are not one clan but a clan that is divided and not strong. If he tries to pass between you and the one standing next to you, move closer together."

"We could hold hands," Wolf said as he reached for Fawn's hand.

50

"No," Ibex whispered. "Do not hold hands, that would appear as if you needed help, or were trying to get strength from the one next to you. Just stand tall and do not let him come between you and the rest of us. If you need to, if he really tries to force his way through, push him back."

"She is right," Fawn said as she spread her legs apart so that she was standing so that more ground was under her body. Her feet were nearly touching those of the feet of Lynx who was on her right side and those of Gesher who was on her left side. "I know these things to be true even if we have never talked of them. I know exile and banishment as a terrible punishment. My memories tell me it is the way of The Chosen."

Lynx looked up at the sky and shook his head. "I also seem to know of this, as Ibex talked the image of being alone formed in my head. It was as if I was dreaming but I know I was awake. I know that exile is a terrible way to punish a person who has done something so wrong that the clan can't allow the person to stay."

Gesher looked at Wolf and Rabbit. "They are of The Chosen by birth, we are of The Chosen by choice. They have abilities that we do not. What they call memories, we would have to be taught. The longer you are a member of this clan the more you will learn of the wonders and abilities of those born to The Chosen."

Fox tapped Rabbit on her shoulder then tried to walk past her. As she felt his gentle push she thrust her elbows out and widened her stance. "No, not here!" She whispered.

Fox turned and took a quick three steps and tried to walk between Fawn and Gesher. "You can't get through here," Gesher said as he twisted around slightly and his arm seemed to accidentally come into contact with the arm of his daughter. "If you want to get to where The Wise One is you will have to go around us, not through us. We will not let you!"

The Wise One saw the line that Ibex and her people had made and a smile seemed to form on his face, then it quickly dissipated as the smile became a frown. "She is indeed a wise leader," he whispered to no one in particular yet to all those gathered around him. "Do not think of her as a woman but as a strong leader."

"But she is a female," Wolverine said.

"Indeed she is," The Wise One answered shaking his head from side to side as he stroked his chin in thought. "A female who is the first to be a leader of a clan of The Chosen. This could be a sign from the spirits of changes that are coming."

"Changes, what kind of changes?" Wolverine asked looking at the man who had been his leader ever since he could remember. "Changes that are good, or changes that are bad?"

"I do not know, only the spirits know what makes changes good or bad. But look at the way her clan does what she asks. They are as one. The Clan of Ibex may be small, just three families but they follow her and do what she says. All the men do as she says."

Fox tried one more time to walk between two of the people standing between where he was and the men of his clan but was pushed back. He did not want to go to where the men were sitting or standing but he had to. He knew he had to do it even if he didn't want to.

"He is coming," Wolverine said, as he saw Fox walk around the edge of the line that Ibex and her clan had formed. "He is coming but his steps are short. He knows he must come here but he doesn't want to do it."

As Fox passed the end of the line he paused for two heartbeats looking at Fawn holding her baby. He saw her smile and then he saw the barely noticeable signals from her fingers. That was all that moved, just her fingers and one hand from the wrist to the fingers. What was that she had just signed? He stood there for a heartbeat trying to think of what she had signaled, then suddenly he understood."

"Yes," he mouthed silently, "I understand."

The Wise One rose to his feet shaking off the help of the men who normally stood by his side helping him to stand or walk. He threw off his protective coverings of skins and stamped his foot on the ground. "Fox, you have broken one of the most sacred customs of our clan, or even of any clan of The Chosen. For that you must be punished. The punishment for a man who breaks the most sacred of our customs is complete exile. From this heartbeat on you are no longer a member of this clan. Take what belongs to you and leave here. Be gone before the moon spirit shows her face."

"No!" The scream came from a young girl, perhaps 8 or 9 springs in age. "You can not send him away."

The girl's mother grabbed her daughter and tried to pull her away. "Marmot, come with me."

"But Fox and I are to be mates. Who will be my mate if he is forced to go into exile?"

"You may be given to another, perhaps from our clan or maybe from another clan, or maybe you will not have a new mate. We must not question the wisdom of our leader or the spirits."

"But," Marmot started to say, then saw the wiggle of Fox's fingers.

"I will say no more," she said as she turned and started to walk away. "If the leader of our clan says Fox must leave then he must leave. The Wise One has been our leader since before you, my mother, were born.

Fox slowly gathered up his few belongings and possessions. He took all of his spears and hand tools. He then rolled his skins into a bundle and threw them over his shoulder. Taking one last look at the members of his clan he started to walk away. One step, then two steps and then he took a third step before he paused to again glance at his people, the ones of his old clan. Not one head was turned toward him. Not one pair of eyes was seeing what he was doing. For a heartbeat he stood there then screamed as loudly as he could. "I am Fox, remember me." Then he turned and ran toward where Ibex and her clan were gathered around their campfires.

"He is coming here." Fawn said. "I did as you asked and sent him a signal saying he would be welcomed into our clan. That he would not be a man without a clan."

"Good," Ibex said quietly. "I know the feeling of despair that being alone can cause. He will be a good member of the Clan of Ibex."

"Mother," Lynx said pointing toward the camp that Fox had been banished from. "Look!"

"I see," Ibex said reaching for a spear. "Perhaps we will have to fight our way out of here after all."

"Who is she?"

"I don't know but watch her. She is sneaking away from the rest of the people and following Fox."

Flashing a sign to Fox, Ibex asked who was following him?

Fox stopped and looked back. Marmot was following him. Little Marmot who had been named as his mate many springs ago was following him. Marmot saw the smile that spread across his face and she broke into a run. "I am coming with you," her signaling and mouthed words told Fox and those watching that she had decided to leave her clan and go with Fox. "Where you are going, I will go also."

"This is Marmot. We were to be named mates at the next full moon," Lynx said as he and Marmot walked into the camp of Ibex and her clan. "She has joined me in my exile, I mean," he said as his face turned just a slight red from embarrassment. "That she and I would like to join your clan and be members of the Clan of Ibex."

"You are both welcome. Come and sit with us." Gesher said as he continued to watch the distant campfires where The Wise One sat with his clan.

"Are they going to come here?" Fawn asked as she too sat and watched the campfires of the Clan of Baranja.

"Soon," Ibex said. "They will be coming soon."

Gesher stood and shielded his eyes from the glare of the setting sun. "It grows dark, soon The Moon Spirit and her Children will wake and The Sun Spirit will sleep."

"I will go to the camp of the Clan of Baranja and talk to The Wise One." Ibex rose to her feet and dropped all of her spears and other weapons onto the ground.

"Wait," Fox said as he jumped to his feet. "You cannot just go there alone. He is the leader of his clan."

"And I am the leader of my clan."

Wolverine saw the activity at the campfires of the Clan of Ibex and nudged The Wise one. "It is time," he said softly. "She is coming here."

"Then leave!" The Wise One said. "It must be just two leaders talking. No others can be here. When two leaders meet to talk, what is said cannot be overheard. When it is time for you to know, you will be told. Be sure that all are where they cannot hear what is said. Have them sit so that they will not be able to see the hand signs and signals. What is said between leaders of clans is between the leaders of the clans."

"I understand," Wolverine said as he motioned for the others to go with him. "May the spirits be with you."

"Come and sit," The Wise One motioned to Ibex. "Why do you come here?"

Ibex knew the formality and responded as custom mandated. "A young female named Marmot has asked to join our clan. She is a member of your clan and you are her leader. I come to ask that she be allowed to join our clan."

"Why would she want to leave the clan that has been her clan since she first drew breath into her lungs?" The Wise One looked right at Ibex without any sign on his face as to what he was thinking.

"She wants to be the mate of a young male who is a member of our clan. She wants to stay with him and be his mate." Ibex looked right back at the old man and did not let her face show any expression or any emotion.

"Who is this young man that she wants to be the mate of?"

"He is called Fox, he wandered into our camp alone."

"I know of no man called Fox. Is he from a clan that calls these mountains theirs?"

"I do not know the clan he is from. Perhaps he is an exile, perhaps he is not!" She said the word with more force to her voice and then made the sign twice. "But we welcomed him to our campfires. Then the young girl followed him. We told her that she also was welcome. But we knew she was a girl of your clan, the Clan of Baranja. If you want her back, then that is your right."

"She is of this clan. But the male she was to be the mate of is no more. If she has found a male in your clan that wants her then that is good. Keep her as a member of your clan."

Ibex rose from where she was sitting. "It is good when two young people find each other. When both are young and healthy the spirits are pleased. Does anyone from your clan wish to talk to her? You and your people are welcome to come and talk to her."

56

"No," The Wise One answered slowly looking directly into Ibex's eyes. "The meeting is over. We have talked, traded and learned from each other. This is our hunting land; it is time for you and your clan to leave. Go and take Marmot with you. I hope that if and when we again meet we will be able to trade and talk."

"I understand," Ibex said. "May the spirits stay with you and your clan and give you many more springs in which to live and see your clan prosper."

"You are indeed a good leader, I thought that a female could never be a leader of any clan of The Chosen. But you have the wisdom and knowledge of a leader. Be careful, leader of the Clan of Ibex. Other clan leaders may not, will not, be as understanding. Watch your back trail."

4

Fox paused at the bend in the river and sent a signal back to the rest of the clan that were following his path. The signs were brief yet urgent. The signals that he sent were first a warning sign then a quiet signal followed immediately by a sign that said someone is coming. Wolf was watching the back trail and was the last to see the signs from Fox.

The small group crouched down on the winding trail that had been trodden down by the hooves of the vast herds of bison and other large animals that traversed the region as they moved from valley to valley looking for newer flourishing pasture.

Fox again sniffed the air and shook his head up and down as he flashed another silent signal back to those behind him. This time the signs said, "I think I smell at least three separate scents."

Gesher took one small step and then two more as he soundlessly moved up to where Fox was crouched. Tapping the young man on the shoulder he smiled and then motioned for him to stand. Leaning over so that his lips were almost touching Fox's ear Gesher whispered to him, "stand up."

"Why?" Fox asked as he glanced at Gesher.

"If we can smell them," Gesher answered quietly, "then they should be able to smell us. Why crouch when it is not needed?"

"Who are you?" The question sounded just beyond the thick vegetation where the trail twisted so that they could not see the people coming toward them.

"We are of the Clan of Ibex," Gesher shouted. "We are searching for people to hunt with and to trade with. We are traveling with our mates and children. Who are you?"

"We are hunters from the Clan of Chapelle," came the reply. "How many are in your group?"

"We are 4 men, their mates and children." Fox shouted, "We have traveled far to find a new home where there is enough game, fresh water, and good caves for our clan."

"You have found what you seek." The voice answered as the first man rounded the curve in the trail then seemed to freeze in place. "A spirit," he shouted as he raised his spear. "It is a spirit come to take us to be with those who have gone before."

Gesher dove behind a thick pine just as the spear thudded into the tree's trunk. "I am not a spirit," he shouted.

"What are you doing?" Ibex lunged at the man and grabbed him by the shoulder. "Why have you attacked him?"

The rest of the clan ran up to where Ibex was just as the rest of the other clan reached the bend in the trail. Fawn saw the spear still quivering in the tree where it had barely missed Gesher and she also saw the look of fear on the man's face. "Calm down," she said quietly as she held out her baby for all to see. "Would a spirit be traveling with females and babies? Would a spirit stand before you talking to you about hunting and trading? We are travelers who are hungry and looking for friends to camp with. If you" she added with just enough anger in her voice to show her displeasure, "are not that clan, then tell us where a clan is that follows the customs of The Chosen and welcomes strangers."

A burley man pushed through the group standing there looking at Ibex and the rest of her clan. "I am called Boar, I am the leader of this hunting party and also the leader of the clan of Chapelle. If the man is really a man why is he so different?"

"He is different that is right, but he is not a spirit," Ibex said sending a signal to Gesher to stand. "Would a spirit be afraid of a spear? Would a spirit hide behind a tree when a spear was thrown at him?"

"I do not know," Boar replied looking at Ibex then at Gesher then forcing his gaze to look at the rest of the strangers standing there. "I have never seen a spirit. The only time one can be sure that he sees a spirit is when he is taken by a spirit to travel to the place where all the spirits of the dead are."

"I am Ibex, the leader of the Clan of Ibex, and I say not only is this man not a spirit but he is my mate."

Boar shook his head from side to side and his eyes seemed to shift slightly as he again looked right at Ibex. "You are of The Chosen, that I can see. So is that man and that woman and also that woman. The male standing by the one you say is your mate looks like one of The Chosen but does not. The rest are not of The Chosen. How can you be a clan of The Chosen if your people are not of The Chosen?"

Wolf moved closer to Gesher. "I am called Wolf and that female standing there is my mate, Rabbit. We were not born to The Chosen as you were. We wanted to be one of The Chosen so we joined Ibex and her clan. Those born to The Chosen have no choice; they are of The Chosen by birth. We did have a choice and we wanted to be members of a clan of The Chosen."

"Boar is our leader," another man said as he moved to stand next to Boar. "A male is the leader of the clan. Not a female. You are not saying what is true. No clan has a female as the leader."

"This one does," Fawn shouted and forced herself to the front of the men. "Ibex leads and we follow. She is the leader of this clan and the men and women listen to her wisdom. She is also my mother." She was about to say more when her baby started to cry.

60

"How can a female be a leader of any clan of The Chosen?" Boar asked as his eyes shifted from Ibex to Gesher then over to Fawn and slowly the rest of those standing by Ibex. "It is not the way of The Chosen. Our customs do not tell of females leading clans."

"I know," Gesher answered slowly as he watched the spears still being held by the men of Boar's hunting party. "When there was just the two of us, Ibex and me, we talked about calling ourselves a clan of The Others and who should be the leader. Ibex did not want to be the leader. She said that in the clans of The Chosen, only men lead. But I told her that where I come from, the lands of The Second People, many of our bands have women as leaders."

"What did you say?" Boar asked as his gaze locked on Gesher. "What are Second People?"

"The Second People are where I came from. You have many clans that make up The Chosen, that is who you are. Wolf, his mate Rabbit and I are from people called The Second People. The bands of The Second People are many and they are traveling this way. They are leaving the homes of our ancestors, following rivers and the edges of the great salt water, they are seeking new hunting lands."

"Why?" Boar asked as his hunters pressed in closer. "Why would anyone want to leave the valleys and mountains that they knew to travel to places they had never been?"

"The Second People follow the trails of the animals that they hunt. They move along the trails that the animals made and follow them wherever they travel. Sometimes they are just a band of hunters; other times they are small family groups of two or three. But they continue to move and seek new places to live as they follow the tracks and trails of their prey." Gesher said, and his hands flew as he also told of the many people moving toward the valleys and mountains that were the ancestral homes of The Chosen.

61

"I do not understand," Boar said yet again as he looked into the faces of his hunters. "Have they hunted the animals until they are no more?"

"No, of course not," Gesher answered trying to think of the words or signs needed to help make them understand. "Perhaps it is just the way of The Second People. They find a new valley or river where the animals are plentiful, they stay for a few springs then become tired of the old place and want to seek new hunting lands."

Boar just shook his head and then turned to the men in his hunting party. "We go," he said signaling them with exaggerated hand signs. "They say they are clan, that they are of The Chosen. But the one with the skin that has no color is strange and I fear he is a spirit. And," he added, glancing back at Ibex, "who ever heard of a clan being led by a female."

Ibex and the rest of her clan stood there watching Boar and his hunting party disappear back down the trail. Wolf shook his head in disbelief. "They have not followed the customs," he muttered more to himself than those gathered around him. "There was no mention of trade or of sharing."

"They were afraid of Gesher," Ibex said.

Rabbit looked at Gesher and nodded, then stepped over to her leader and put her arm around Ibex's shoulder. "I know," she whispered softly. "It is not the way of The Chosen or of The Second People. Both welcome strangers and try to make them happy in their camps. We were not even invited to go with them."

Fawn watched Boar and his hunters disappear around the curve in the trail. "If that is the way they want to be, not even offering the tiniest piece of meat, or even an offer to trade, then they are not the type of people we want to be with. It is hard to think that they are people of The Chosen."

"Let them go," Wolf shouted at the retreating backs. "Real men and women, those who follow the customs, would not want to be with them."

Boar stopped walking and held up his arm in the one signal all people knew. It said simply "stop!"

Boar had stopped so quickly that the hunter right behind him almost walked into his back.

"We have to go back," Boar said in a whisper. "The spirits would not be happy with us if we did not follow the customs and invite them to come with us on our hunt. We did not even offer them meat. Have I have offended the spirits? Will they refuse us the prey that we hunt?"

"But it is the spring," the hunter said glancing first at Boar then back up the trail where the strangers were. "The bear cubs are coming out of the dens. We always hunt the cave bear cubs and those that are one spring old when the last of the snow melts and the streams again flow."

"That is right," Boar said as he turned and started back up the trail. "But we may have made the spirits angry when we refused to show the strangers that they were welcome. To make the spirits angry is not good to do."

The slight snapping of a twig made Lynx turn his head and glance toward the bend in the trail. He was watching the back trail as the clan began walking back the way they had come. He reached out and tapped Fawn on the back. "Smell the air, they are coming back. Let the others know."

Fawn paused for the briefest of a heartbeat, then took two quick steps and touched Wolf. "Boar and the others are coming back. Let Gesher and Ibex know."

Ibex stopped when the whispered voice reached her ears. "If they are coming back, that is good."

Marmot reached out and grabbed the hand of her mate. "Fox, I am afraid. Why are they coming back?"

Fox put his arm around her shoulder and pulled her close. "See how Gesher and Ibex are just standing there? They are not afraid. There is no fear in their stance, no fear in their faces. Watch and learn my little Marmot."

As Boar turned the edge of the curve, he yelled out. "Ibex are you there? It is I Boar and my hunting party. I ask that you, and the spirits forgive me for the way I treated you and your clan. Perhaps I was so worried about hunting the cave bear cubs that I forgot the customs. Would you and your people want to join us in our hunt?"

"Did you say you were hunting cave bear cubs?" Wolf asked, as he pushed past Rabbit to stand in front of her and the baby.

"Yes," Boar said gesturing toward the high mountain to the right. "When the last of the snows melt off the high peaks of the mountain, and the rivers and streams fill with the fresh water, we go and hunt for the new born cave bear cubs and those that were born one spring ago. The meat is tender and the fat, when it is boiled, makes a covering for our skins that keeps most biting bugs from biting us."

Gesher glanced quickly at Ibex. "I never heard of boiling bear fat to keep bugs from biting. I would like to learn more."

"It is also something I never knew," Ibex said as she began to slowly walk toward Boar. "On behalf of the Clan of Ibex, I say this. We would like to join you and your hunters on this hunt. It is something we did not know. We thank you for the opportunity to join you and to learn a new hunting skill. You have offered us a great gift. What can my clan offer you?"

Boar's face started to turn red. He had not thought that the invitation to go on a hunt would be thought of as a gift. He had not been prepared to offer anything except the opportunity to join them on a hunt. Now Ibex had said it was a great gift. What could he ask for from them? This female, this leader of the can of Ibex, had surprised him with her skill of knowing the lore and customs of The Chosen. What could he ask for that would be the same?

Ibex realized that Boar was suddenly quiet and thoughtful. The thought of what she had said, that the idea of putting boiled bear fat on their skin to keep biting insects away, was something that they did not know. That was bothering Boar. What could she do to make him feel better?

"Boar," she said quietly as she sent him and his hunters a quick series of signs. "My clan is getting a great gift from you, a new way of doing something that we did not know about, a way of using the fat of a bear to keep the biting insects away. Trade is the way of The Chosen. My clan must now give you something in return, something that has a value that is the same as what you gave us. We know that The Chosen are meat eaters. That they like to hunt the large animals of the forests and the plains. But we have a new type of spear, one that has a barb on the point where it is hafted to the shaft. It keeps small animals from slipping off the spear and can also be used to spear the great sturgeon in the rivers. I would like to give you two of these new spears. Then your skilled tool makers can copy the point."

Boar looked at Ibex and then smiled. "It is a good trade. The spirits will be pleased."

"Then will you lead us?" Ibex asked in a very quiet voice. "I and my clan will follow you. You are the one who knows the secrets of the caves where the bears are to be found."

Boar looked at Ibex and the rest of her clan standing there. "The males can come, but you and the other females, along with the babies must seek shelter and stay there. Hunting a cave bear is dangerous. The female cave bear, with or without cubs, is very dangerous. If a male cave bear sees us, a fully-grown adult male, it will be extremely dangerous. One swipe from his paw could gut a man from the chest to the hips. It could also take his head off his shoulders. Hunting cave bear is for men, not women."

"Ibex is a hunter," Gesher said with just enough anger in his voice to make even Ibex's head turn toward him. "Let me tell you about her and her skills. For many moons, I mean springs; I wandered alone though unknown places. Then I found Ibex and we began to travel together. It was Ibex who told me of the cave lion. We hunted where the cave lion made a kill. We faced the death that the cave lion could bring, but we lived. Have you heard of the Terrible One? Just four of us, Ibex, Lynx and Fawn found a pride of the Terrible ones in an open treeless valley. One of them attacked us. But we faced it together and killed it. Fawn was a young girl, not yet old enough to be called a woman. But her courage was equal to mine. She drove her spear into the chest of the Terrible One as it leapt at my throat. The females of our clan are as brave and fearless as any male. I trust any of them with my life."

Boar's eyes were as wide open as they could be. "You saw the animal called the Terrible One?"

"No, we did not." Gesher said shaking his hand in the gesture that was almost an insult. "We saw three of them and one of them attacked us. We killed it as it made its last massive jump toward our throats. It fell dead at our feet. If we had been one step closer, but I do not think, or worry, about such things."

"Three of them?" Boar asked in a whisper. "The Terrible One is the killer of all killers. If you faced three and killed one, then you are indeed hunters that have no fear. All of you are welcome to join our hunting party. We welcome your spears and your courage."

"Thank you Boar, we will join you," Ibex said grasping his hand. "But the women with babies should stay behind. If one of the babies started to cry just as we came near our prey, it would alert it and spoil the stalk and the hunt. Is there a place close to here where the two mothers and their babies could stay? One that is safe and yet close to fresh running water? One of their mates, or even both, could stay to watch out for danger."

"Yes, there is. I know of a cave that is exactly what you say is needed. We can stop there before continuing the hunt."

"There is the cave," Boar signed as he pointed toward the small opening in the face of the cliff. It is very small on the outside; a man has to bend down to walk in. You would have to get down on your hands and knees and crawl in. But it is deep, nearly a full spear throw from front to back. The stream that runs past it is deep and only a few paces from the entrance. One person could protect the entrance against any animal."

Ibex stood there for many heartbeats looking at the small narrow entrance and the stream rushing past. Then she turned and went inside. The glow from her burning torch cast long shimmering shadows on the walls as she carefully moved deeper into the cave.

"Good," she finally said as she turned and started back toward the tiny opening that was the entrance to the cave. "It is a good place for the mothers and their babies to stay. But I think that both of their mates should stay here with them. That way one of the men can stay on watch while the other sleeps or sits with his mate. Then they can switch and the one guarding the entrance can go to be with his mate while the one who was snuggling with his mate goes to stand watch."

"But I want to go, I want to hunt the cave bear, Lynx said as he picked up his spears.

"No, you are staying!" Ibex said. "And so is Wolf."

"But," was all that Lynx was able to say when the glare from Gesher made him shut his mouth.

Fawn and Rabbit sat at the entrance to the cave with their babies suckling at their breasts. Lynx sat next to Fawn and chipped away at a new piece of flint that he was slowly shaping into a spear point. Standing barely two steps further Wolf watched the hunters disappear into the overgrowth that seemed to hide the twisting trail. He waived briefly, and then took the long thick nut tree branch that he was bending into a straight shaft for his spear. Holding it out at arm's length, he shut the left eye and looked down the shaft with his right eye. "It still needs to be straightened just a little more," he said more to himself than those gathered around him. "I think I will go and soak it in the stream until the sun goes down. Then it should be supple enough to put in the shaft straightener while we sleep. By the time The Sun Spirit wakes, it should be ready to fit onto my new point."

Marmot reached out to the baby as Fawn finished suckling it. She had decided to stay back with the other two young women. "Can I hold the baby? I will be gentle and watchful."

"Yes, of course you can," Fawn said as she handed the infant to the young girl. "Have you ever held a baby before?"

"No, the mothers were very protective of their babies. No other female other than the mother, and those women who are of the mother's hearth or a close hearth, can hold a baby."

"Well in the Clan of Ibex, babies can be held by anyone who wants to hold them. Males or females, young or old, same hearth or not, we are all one in this clan. Babies are the men and women of the springs yet to come. Without babies our clan, the Clan of Ibex would be no more. It is good practice for young girls and even boys to learn how to hold a baby and to attend to the baby's wants."

Wolf glanced up and then back down to continue working on his spear point. But as he turned the blade over he felt a gentle touch on his arm. "Wolf," his mate whispered in his ear. "The baby is sleeping. Why not come with me and we can make love under the trees. It has been three days since you held me close and we made love. I want you!"

"There is what we have been looking for," Boar whispered as he signaled the group of hunters to stop. "That is the track of a cave bear! It seems to be that of an animal that is one spring old, or maybe two springs old, but definitely not a fully grown cave bear."

"It must be that of a two spring old," the older hunter from Boar's clan said. "If it was only one spring old, it would still be traveling with the female that was its mother.

Boar nodded silently. "That is true Hawk. The young stay with the mother until they are two springs in age. Then the female forces the cub to leave so that she can mate again and have more cubs. This bear is alone. That means it is two springs in age. The fat would be better but the meat tougher to chew. What do you think? Should we follow the trail of this animal or continue to hunt for another?"

Hawk stood there slowly studying the paw marks. He dropped down on his hands and knees and inhaled slowly. He took a small handful of the dirt where the bear had left a footprint and licked it. He then placed it on his tongue and tasted it. "It is old, at least one day has passed since this track was made. The bear could be two or more ridges away by now. We should look for fresher sign. Keep looking for tracks of at least two animals traveling together, one larger than the other. That would be a cub and the mother."

"Good!" Boar said, "we will look beyond this track."

Ibex glanced at Gesher and Fox. "Hawk is very good. Few trackers can taste the track and tell how long ago the animal passed by."

"You can, I have seen you do it," Gesher said almost silently to his mate. "You are just as good as he is."

"Hush," she replied as her finger touched her lips in the be-silent sign.

The Sun Spirit was seeking his sleeping place in the west as the hunters trudged the ridge. Boar and Ibex were leading the group while Gesher and Fox stayed back watching the back trail. "It will soon be dark," Ibex signed silently. "Is there any place, perhaps a cave or secure rock formation, where we can spend the night? The Sun Spirit is sleepy and the Moon Spirit is not yet awake. Soon it will be dark and we will not be able to see."

"No," Boar signed. "But we should be close to the den of a cave bear. I have been catching a faint scent on the breeze when it blows from where the Sun Spirit wakes."

"East," Ibex signed. "In our clan we call the place where the Sun Spirit wakes east and where he sleeps west."

Boar and Hawk took a few heartbeats to glance at Ibex. "You have to tell us more of what your clan says and does. I think your clan has more to teach us than you have said." Boar sent her a fast smile then again took up the trail.

A shout from Gesher made all the hunters stop and turn their eyes back down the trail. "Bear," he shouted. "A big one, and it is coming this way!"

Boar turned where he was and ran back to where Gesher and Fox were standing. "Where?"

"Fox saw it for one heartbeat. I think I saw it but maybe I did not. But it is big and coming this way. It is following our tracks. It is tracking us!"

Ibex glanced at Boar. "We are in the middle of a trail. There is thick forest on both sides. You have hunted these cave bears before. What is your plan?"

"We have to get off the trail," Boar almost shouted. "Look for a tree to climb or a high rocky ledge. It is death to stay here and face the charge of a fully-grown cave bear. Run for your life."

As Boar and his hunters started to run, a voice seemed to stop them. "No," Gesher shouted as he knelt in the middle of the path.

"We live or die here! To try to outrun the bear is impossible. To face it alone is death. But if we all stay here and face the onslaught as one we may survive."

Ibex drove the butt of her spear into the ground with the point facing toward where the cave bear should appear. "I am staying. Gesher and I faced the Terrible One and killed it. We will face the attack of the cave bear together."

"I am here," Fox said as he hefted his spear and felt for the best balance along the thick shaft. His other hand held another spear in the jabbing position. "I stand with my leader and her mate."

Hawk saw the three hunters from Ibex's clan kneeling and standing there waiting for the rush of the cave bear. "You will need a fourth person. I will stay. My spears and club are ready."

The young male from Boar's clan, the one who they now knew was called Snake, shifted his weight on his feet as he looked at his leader and then at Ibex and Gesher along with Fox and Hawk. "If you are staying I am staying. I have three spears."

Boar shook his head. "What are you thinking? How can you face the attack of a cave bear on a narrow game trail? There is barely enough space between the overhanging limbs to throw your spears."

"There is a saying that our people have," Gesher said quietly. "The saying is something that is right to say now as we get ready to face death from the cave bear. The saying is simple. When death is certain, turn and face it. Do not let death find your back. Face it!"

Boar looked at Gesher. "It is a good saying. I will stay and face death with you."

The cracking of a limb off to their right made Ibex turn her head. "The bear may circle us. There are six of us here. I think that we should have two hunters kneeling with their spears in the jabbing position. Then two more standing right behind them with their

71

spears ready to throw. The other two should stand with their shoulders touching the two who are standing but with their feet turned so that they are watching the sides. Gesher and I are already kneeling. I want Fox and Hawk to be in back of us with their spears ready to throw. Boar, you and your other hunter watch our sides looking for the bear if it circles around. If anyone actually sees the bear, yell so that we all are facing where it is."

"There it is," Fox screamed. "It is massive and coming right up the trail."

The large cave bear paused as he saw the puny things blocking his path. As he reared up on his back legs to get a better look at whatever it was that was in his way to the berry patch, which he knew was just behind the next hill, two spears thudded into his chest. One imbedded itself in his large heart and the other in his lung.

His roar was a blend of pain and anger. But even as the roar erupted from his chest two more spears thudded into his thick muscular body. One slipped past the ribs protecting his liver and split it nearly in half. The other struck his neck just above the shoulders. Dropping back down onto all four paws he lunged toward the place where he had seen the puny things in his path. Even as he lurched forward, two more spears struck him. One hit him in the face just above his right eye and the blood that flowed out of the wound filled his eye so he couldn't see out of it. The other sliced into his shoulder and cut the tendon.

He wobbled slightly as his one shoulder collapsed under him but he continued his attack on the remaining three legs. One more massive leap and he was on top of the people in his way. His paw slapped out and thudded into the arm of Fox. The scream from Fox as the claws ripped flesh from his arm was awful.

Gesher lunged forward and drove his spear into the bear's broad neck. The blood from the severed jugular spurted out and covered Gesher from his face to his waist.

Ibex yelled as she sprang at the bear and drove her spear into the gapping snarling mouth and felt the spear stick in the roof of the bear's mouth. Then watched as the jaws snapped shut severing the shaft in two.

The bear reared up on his two hinds legs and his paw ripped across the chest of Boar leaving four deep lacerations on the man's body running from just below the right shoulder down to his belly.

Hawk paused for the briefest of heartbeats then he jumped forward and drove his one remaining spear deep into the bear's soft under belly and then twisted it as hard as he could upward into the chest cavity.

The bellow from the massive male reverberated off the trees and brush. His paw smashed the shaft of the spear into nothing but thin slivers of wood. The blood spurted from his mouth and nose as he fought to breathe. He dropped back down onto his three remaining legs just a heartbeat before Gesher's heavy club shattered the bone of his other front leg.

"He is down," Boar shouted. "Both front legs are useless. He can't stand up and the wounds that he has will soon kill him."

"He is waiting for death," Ibex said watching the bear for a heartbeat before turning to the wounded hunters. "Boar how deep are the claw marks on your chest? There is a lot of blood running down your chest but I see you are not having any problems breathing. That means that there is no injury to your lungs."

"They are not deep, but they may bring the spirits here that make those with injuries sick. I wish that we had brought our medicine woman with us."

"I am a medicine woman," Ibex said as she turned to see how Fox was and what his injuries were. "And Gesher is a healer. Gesher can treat your wounds while I look at Fox and his wounds."

"Fox, how bad is it?" Ibex asked as she knelt next to the young man. "The Cave bear caught your arm with his claws, I saw that, but is it serious?"

"I can't feel my fingers."

Ibex's quick glance told Gesher that it was serious. "As soon as you are finished with Boar I need your help! Someone needs to get my traveling medicine bag and spread the medicines out on a skin."

"The cave bear is not dead, we can not skin him yet."

"Then peel off your clothes, get the clothes off the others also. Spread the skins on the ground and empty all my medicines onto the skins. I need to see what I have in large amounts. Do it now!" she almost screamed, but held her growing panic in check.

As the various medicines were spread out on the skins that were the clothes of the hunters, Ibex and Gesher began to sort through them.

"He needs to remain calm," Gesher whispered to his mate. "We have more than enough Humulus along with Bee Balm and Nepeta to put him to sleep."

"And there appears to be enough Bramble, Boneset and Bloodwort," Ibex whispered back.

"The Verbena is low, we should look for more as soon as we can," Gesher added as he looked over the mounds of various stems, leaves, flowers, roots, bulbs and other forms of vegetation that they used as their medicines.

"First we have to wash the wound. Any dirt, any piece of clothing, even a small loose piece of flesh has to be gotten out of the wound."

"Fox," Gesher said softly as he signaled to the others that were clustered around the young man. You should not be standing. You should be lying down."

Ibex slowly poured the contents of her water skins over the arm of Fox. She used all three of her water carriers and then signaled Gesher for his and emptied both of his as she gently rubbed the long deep lacerations. "I think I have all the dirt and loose skin removed," she said nearly silently. But those gathered around her heard the way she said it. It was not only Gesher who heard the slight sound of worry in her words. Fox heard and looked up at the leader of his clan. "If the arm must be cut off so that I can live to be the mate of Marmot and the Dada of her children, then that is what the spirits want. Give me the medicine that will make me sleep so that I will not cry out or move my arm as you sever it from my shoulder."

"You are a brave man for one so young," Hawk said as he sat down by Fox.

Boar walked slowly over to where Ibex and Gesher were setting up the piles of medicine plants. "Fox is indeed a brave man; to be ready to have his arm cut off is very brave. The Chosen, and you have said many times that your clan is of The Chosen, care for those that are too injured to care for themselves. But if you do not want to care for Fox after his arm is cut off, do not abandon him. My clan will take him in. A man as brave as he is deserves to live even if he can no longer hunt."

"As will the Clan of Ibex," Gesher replied in a whisper. "If he is injured so badly that he must have an arm cut off to save his life, then he will be cared for by the clan for as long as he lives. He will not have to hunt for meat, he will not have to make flint tools, and he will not need anything in order to live. What he needs will be provided by the clan. That is the way of all people!"

"Will you two be quiet!" Ibex said as she twisted the arm in order to look at it. As she bent it backward, Fox moaned then screamed in pain. "Gesher, prepare the medicines to make him sleep. I don't want to do what is needed until he is unaware of what I am doing. It has to be the sleep that lasts until the Sun Spirit wakes."

Gesher pulled out the Boneset and placed it on the skins next to Fox. "As soon as he is no longer aware of what we are doing, the Boneset to treat his wounds is ready."

Boar stood there watching Ibex and Gesher as they made their medicines for Fox. There was a fire burning for the plants that needed to be boiled to release the benefits they carried. Those plants that did not need to be boiled were either being crushed in order to make the medicines available that were hidden within their roots, leaves or stems. Suddenly he pointed and then a smile began to spread across his face. "The moon is beginning to wake. The full face of the moon is showing. Soon we will have enough light to see without even a fire."

Ibex paused for a heartbeat and she also let a smile briefly dance on her lips. "The spirits are kind. Soon I will be able to see the damage caused by the claws of the bear." She paused and looked directly at Gesher. "But I do not think I can save the arm."

"We will do what we can," Gesher said shaking his head. "But the spirits are the ones who know what will happen."

Boar grabbed Hawk and then Snake. "We can build fires. Get as much limbs, branches and even thick trunks. Build one up the trail and one down the trail. With fires at both sides of where Ibex and Gesher are helping Fox, no animal will come near. The fires may even help them see what has to be done. The moon is now above the horizon, but the trees will hide it for a long while. It is up to the three of us to make the fires and to stand guard. Go now, and be swift."

The fires blazing on both sides of Fox added to the slowly rising moon that began to illuminate the place where Fox lay. "He is nearly asleep," Gesher said quietly as he tilted Fox's head back and tried to force more of the sleeping medicines down him. "Drink," he kept saying, "drink more."

"The wound is very bad," Ibex said as she began to examine the wound caused by the claws of the cave bear as they ripped pieces of flesh, muscle and bone form the upper arm of Fox. "The tendons are torn in two, the muscle is in shreds and the bone is splintered. There is no way that the arm can be saved. I have to cut it off at the shoulder." She shook her head as just one tiny tear dripped from the corner of her eye.

"He is young and he is strong," Gesher said as he signaled to Boar and his hunters. "If the spirits want, he will live. His fate is in their hands." Then he paused for only a heartbeat and then added, "and your hands."

"He is sleeping the sleep of those who have a belly full of the sleeping drink," Ibex said as she shifted some of her medicines so that some were very close. "I need a big fire, one that gives off enough light so that I can see without any shadows. And I will need as many sharp cutting blades as possible. Does anyone have a large hammer stone with them?"

"I do," Snake said.

"Give it to me," Ibex whispered. "I need it to break the remaining bones in his arm."

Gesher got up from where he was sitting. "Even though he is sleeping the sleep of those with a belly full of the sleeping medicines, he will move as Ibex cuts his arm. We need to hold him down. Boar take his right arm, I will take the left arm. Hawk you sit on the right leg and Snake you on the left leg. He must not be able to move as Ibex amputates his arm."

Ibex looked at the four men holding Fox. "Are you all ready? I need him to be as still as you can make him. No matter what happens, do not release a leg or arm. Boar, you have the right arm, the one I am cutting off. You need to hold him higher, up by the shoulder. You have the most responsibility. That is the arm that must not move. Now does anyone need to do anything before I start?"

All four men shook their heads from side to side. "Do it now," Gesher said.

"Yes," Snake added. "Do it now."

"The flesh is ripped almost off the arm here," Ibex said as she cut away at the dangling strips of Fox's upper arm. "The muscle is completely off the bone and the tendons ripped in pieces. I need to amputate the arm right at the shoulder joint. As soon as I have cut all the skin, flesh and muscle off, I will use the hammer stone to hit the end of the sharp skinning blade that will separate the upper arm from the shoulder. It may take many blows from the hammer stone on the blunt end of the skinning blade before it breaks the two bones apart. That is when he will move the most, or try to move."

"Do it!" Gesher whispered as he bore down on Fox's shoulder and arm with all his strength. "Now!"

Holding the hammer stone in her right hand, Ibex placed the thin skinning blade against the point where the two bones were joined. The sharp point of the skinning blade was pressed firmly at the place where Ibex was certain the bones could be separated the easiest. "Spirits help me," she whispered and then swung the hammer stone downward. The blunt end of the hammer stone struck the blunt ends of the skinning blade driving the point into the joint. Ibex lifted the heavy stone again and brought it down. The joint slowly opened and the arm fell to the ground as it separated from the shoulder. "Now," Ibex nearly shouted as the blood spurted from Fox's severed shoulder. "Bring me the spear that is in the fire."

Boar leapt up and grabbed the spear that Ibex had put in the fire. "The shaft is nearly burnt through," he told her as he handed it to her. "Be careful that it does not break."

The smell of burning flesh seemed to permeate the night air as Ibex pressed the red hot blade of the spear against the open wound that was the place where Fox's shoulder used to be attached to his arm. "The hot blade will sear the wound and stop it from bleeding. But the burn will need much attention. It is good that we have enough medicine plants to treat both burns and pain."

"More than enough," Gesher added as he began to make up a thick glob to spread on the seared flesh. "But have you thought about how we are going to get him back to where the rest are? It will be many days until he can even begin to walk."

Ibex straightened her back by arching backward as she pressed on her waist. "I haven't even begun to worry about that. For the next two days the only worry I will have is keeping Fox alive. I do not know how much blood was lost before I was able to sear the wound shut with fire."

Hawk tapped Ibex on the shoulder then leaned closer. "Fox can't go to where Marmot and the others are staying but they could come here."

"Yes, of course they could." Ibex said, smiling up at the hunter. "Would you go and bring the rest of the clan here?"

"I will go as soon as the light from the Sun Spirit shows on the horizon."

5

Fawn was the one who was watching the trail when Hawk reached the bend in the path. Her cry of delight brought the rest out of the tiny cave. "They are coming," she shouted. "There is Hawk, he is in the lead, and there comes Snake."

Marmot stood there by Fawn for a heartbeat then glanced at Lynx. "Where are the rest? Why is there only two?"

"They must be further behind. They must be carrying the hide, fat and meat from a bear." Lynx told her as he began to walk toward the returning hunters. "Were you able to slay one or two?"

But it was Rabbit who first felt the rush of fear deep in her stomach. "Something has happened," she screamed as the realization that there were only two men returning and not the whole hunting party. "Where are the rest? What has happened?"

Hawk stopped as the group rushed toward him. "Gather up your traveling packs. A big male cave bear injured Fox. Ibex and Gesher have stopped the bleeding and are caring for him. But he can't walk back this far. Ibex sent us to bring you."

"Fox was hurt?" Marmot asked as she grabbed Hawk by the arm. "How did it happen? Why did they not flee from a big cave bear? Is it," she started to ask, and then stopped as she slowly began to understand what Hawk had said. Fox could not walk back! "Where is he," she murmured softly tugging at Hawk's arm. "I have to go to him."

"We will all go," Fawn said pulling the young girl toward her and hugging her. "As soon as we can pick up all of our packs and other belongings we will go to them."

"How bad is it," Wolf asked as he walked past where Hawk was sitting chewing on a bison leg.

"Bad," was all that Hawk answered but the glance said more.

"Wolf hurried and put the remaining blades and partially finished spear points in his two packs. "As soon as Hawk and Snake have had some food and rest we can leave."

"We are ready now," Snake replied throwing his traveling pack over his shoulder. "We should get there as quickly as we can."

"Why?" Marmot asked looking the young man right in the eye as she asked the question. "You still have not answered any questions as to how serious the injury is. Is it a broken leg? Or," she added as an image entered her mind. "Did he hurt his head or eyes?"

"We must go now!" Hawk added quietly as he started back down the path. "Ibex said to come here and bring the rest of the clan."

"But how bad is the wound?" Fawn asked as she began trekking down the trail.

"Wolf, you take the back trail," Lynx said as he fell into step behind Hawk. "Snake will stay with you. I think we should have two men in the back watching our back trail while Hawk and I are leading and watching in front."

"Yes, that is a good idea," Hawk said as he glanced back over his shoulder at the people following him. "That is how the cave bear attacked us. It was tracking us!"

"Tracking you?"

"Gesher shouted something about seeing a big cave bear. That he thought it was following our tracks. That it was tracking us as if it was hunting us."

"Carnivores track us, at least sometimes they do. The big cats sometimes cut our trail and begin to hunt us. But the cave bear is not a carnivore; it does not live on meat. It prefers to eat fruit and other vegetation." Lynx said as his head swiveled from side to side while his eyes searched for any danger. "That is why we always have someone watching the back trail."

"Gesher and Fox were watching the back trail. They were the first to see, or at least sense the bear. It was Gesher who told us to stop and face death, that we could not outrun the bear. We stood and waited for the attack. Ibex and Gesher were in front kneeling with their spears in the jabbing position. The rest of us were standing and had our spears ready to throw."

"It was a good plan," Lynx said as he thought of the man who was his father. "Gesher is wise in the ways of the animals."

"Yes it was a good plan. He was right. The bear would have caught us one by one if we had run. By standing together we fought the bear and won. By now he is skinned and the fat is being boiled. At least I hope that someone is boiling the fat. I would not want to think that Fox lost his arm and we lost the fat."

Lynx reached out to grab Hawk but then stopped as he realized that Marmot was only a few paces behind and he did not want to alarm her. "Fox lost an arm?"

"The cave bear was severely wounded, we had thrown many spears and they were all in fatal places. But the bear still attacked. It lunged forward and struck Fox with his massive paw. He ripped the flesh from Fox's arm and tore huge chunks of skin and muscle from the bone. Ibex cut the arm off to save his life."

"She cut off his arm?" Lynx whispered so softly that he barely heard the question himself. "Which arm and where was it cut off?"

"It was his right arm, and she had to cut it off at the shoulder."

"At the shoulder?"

"Yes, she used a hammer stone to drive a sharp skinning blade into the joint to separate it after cutting off the skin and muscle. Then she burned the wound to keep the blood in the body."

"Now I understand why you kept what had happened to Fox from his mate."

"She is a female of The Chosen, she knows the dangers of hunting," Hawk whispered back. "Females of The Chosen do not question why the spirits do what they do. She will understand."

"Yes, but Marmot is young and she has just become the mate of Fox. She left her clan to join ours and be his mate."

"But she is of The Chosen!"

"Yes, she is," Lynx acknowledged, "and she will not shame our clan or The Chosen by her actions."

Fawn caught up to the two men and heard just enough of what they were talking about to make her want to hear more. "What did you just say?"

"We were just talking," Lynx said glancing at her.

"No, you were saying something about not shaming the clan or The Chosen. Why would you say that?"

"Fawn," Lynx whispered to his mate, "can't two men just want to talk without having to explain?"

"You hear everything I say," she answered glaring at him. "What is it that you are saying that you are trying to keep me, and the others, from hearing?"

"We were just talking about hunting and how exciting it is," Lynx said under his breath.

"No, you were saying something else," Fawn replied nudging her mate with her elbow. "You would not be whispering and trying to hide your signs if you were only talking about hunting. Why are you telling me things that are not true?"

"You are right," Lynx sent the sign as he silently mouthed the words. "Fox has been injured by a full grown male cave bear. It was tracking the hunting party and then attacked them. Fox has injuries on the arm; the wound so severe that Ibex had to amputate it."

"Is he still alive?" Fawn signed back.

"He was when Snake and Hawk were sent back to get us."

"We should tell Marmot."

"No, Gesher said not to say anything."

"She is his mate, she needs to know."

"But Gesher said not to say anything."

"If anything happened to you, I would want to know. Marmot is Fox's mate, she should know."

"But," Lynx started to say, but Fawn was already headed back to where Marmot was walking.

As Fawn passed Rabbit she sent a very short but urgent series of signs to Rabbit. She had waited until Marmot was not watching exactly where she was going but instead had shifted her gaze for only a heartbeat or perhaps two, to the side of the trail.

Rabbit nodded and stopped to shift the baby from one arm to the other. "Hi Marmot," she smiled at the young girl as Marmot passed her on the path. "How are you doing?"

Marmot paused and glanced at Rabbit and then noticed that Fawn was also standing very close to where they were. "Why have we stopped?" The question, and quiver in her voice, seemed to carry more of a sound of worry than just a normal question of inquiry.

"Marmot," Fawn said as she moved closer to the young woman, "you need to know that Fox was severely injured by the cave bear. That is why we are going to where he is."

Marmot looked at Fawn then her eyes traveled to where Lynx and Hawk were standing. "Yes, they told me. But is there something I was not told?"

"He was in the front of the hunters as the cave bear attacked. The bear's claws tore his right arm. Ibex and Gesher did all that they could. Remember that Ibex is a medicine woman of The Chosen and Gesher is a healer. But they had to amputate his arm at the shoulder. There was nothing else that they could do."

Marmot stood there for many heartbeats, perhaps as many as ten or more before saying anything. Then she looked at Hawk. "Is he still living?"

"He was alive when we left. Ibex is giving him medicines to make him sleep and for the pain."

"Well don't just stand there staring at me, get going. My mate will need me at his side to care for his wounds."

Fawn smiled as she glanced at her mate. The sign she flashed to him said more than many words could have. The sign said simply what she wanted to say. It was a one-word message. "See!

The Sun Spirit was slowly sinking in the west when Hawk called a stop. "It is getting dark and we still have some distance to travel. We should stop here for the night and start again in the morning."

"No, we need to still travel," Marmot said as she pushed to the front. "I want to be with Fox as soon as I can. He needs me."

"It is not safe to walk unknown trails in the dark," Lynx told her as he let his traveling packs slide off his shoulders.

"It is not safe to face the attack of a cave bear, or to hunt carnivores, but we do." Marmot said.

"There is no light to see where we are walking," Wolf added as he sat down of the edge of the trail. "Now is not the time to stumble in the dark and break a leg."

"But we could start up again as soon as there is light from The Moon Spirit," Rabbit told them, as she sat down and started to suckle her baby.

"We could," Wolf said, and plopped down next to his mate.

"Then that is what we will do," Fawn said, tugging on Lynx's arm, "won't we?"

"Well, we should try to get some sleep," Lynx told them as he sprawled out on the edge of the trail. "If, when The Moon Spirit does shine tonight, and, if there is enough light to travel by, there will be enough light to wake us."

Marmot nudged Lynx. "The Moon Spirit is awake and there is more than enough light to see where our feet are stepping. I want to get to Fox as quickly as possible. Let's wake the others and be on our way."

Fawn rolled over and looked up at the young girl standing over her. She propped herself up on an elbow and looked at The Moon Spirit and her Children. "I think that there is enough light too."

Lynx looked at his mate and then at Marmot before again glancing up at the star filled sky. "If we do go, and I am still not sure it is a good idea, we will have to walk slowly and carefully. In the almost dark, a misstep on an unseen rock, or tripping on a small log could cause a broken leg or worse."

"I think it is a chance we should take," Fawn told her mate. "It is important that Marmot get to Fox as soon as she can."

"I understand, but I am still worried. Why not wait until the first glow from the waking Sun Spirit is seen on the horizon?"

"Because Marmot is worried," Fawn said.

Hawk stirred in his sleeping skins and opened his eyes. "What is wrong? Is it my turn to stand guard already?"

"No," Lynx whispered back. "Marmot and Fawn want to start the journey back to where Fox and the others are."

"I don't think that there is enough light," Hawk muttered as he rolled over.

"Yes there is," Marmot said, and her voice had more than a little hint of anger mixed with frustration.

"Yes there is," Fawn agreed.

Lynx looked at his mate then at Marmot and shrugged. "Wake the others and we will go."

The Sun Spirit was nearly at the highest point he would travel when Hawk paused on the trail. "When we left to come back and get you, we left them about three spear throws from here. They should be there unless they moved."

Marmot looked at him then at Fawn. "I want to see him, if he is alive or with the spirits, I want to see him now!"

Ibex glanced up from where she was slowly dripping medicines into Fox's mouth. "They are here," she softly said to those gathered around her and Fox.

Gesher's momentary look up the trail before he again started to prepare the medicines for Fox made the rest of the people pause and look at the group nearly running toward them.

Marmot was the first to reach the place where Fox lay. "Is he?" She started to ask then stopped as she saw his chest slowly expand as another breath of air filled his lungs. "He is!" Her yell reverberated through the small opening where they were gathered. "He is still alive!"

Dropping down on the ground beside her mate she reached out and brushed the hair from in front of his eyes. "Fox," she whispered as her hands lightly caressed his face, "I am here." She paused for a heartbeat then leaned close to his ear. "I love you, do not leave me. I want to be a mother. I want you to be the Dada of our baby."

"He can't hear you. " Gesher said as he tried to help her back up. "Ibex has been giving him medicines for the pain and to make him sleep. If he did wake he would be in much pain."

Marmot sat there running her hands over his face. "He is hot, I can feel fever."

"Yes," Gesher said as he handed more medicines to Ibex. "Ibex is giving him medicines for that too."

"Where is the arm?" Marmot asked, as her gaze swept the area. "Where is Fox's arm?"

Gesher and Boar looked at each other. It was Gesher who finally answered her. "We buried it."

"Buried it?" Marmot asked looking right at the mate of her leader.

"If someone dies, they are buried." Boar replied. "He is clan and the arm was buried according to clan customs. Do not worry about the arm. We did the burial ceremony for the arm just like we would if it was someone who had died."

"Thank you," Marmot whispered.

Lynx and Fawn sat down next to where Ibex was. "When did you last sleep?" Fawn asked noticing the red eyes and slow reflexes that Ibex had.

"I will sleep when the spirits tell me that Fox is going to live."

"You can't continue to stay awake. What if you give him a wrong medicine? You need to get some sleep."

"No, I am a medicine woman of The Chosen. The spirits made me a medicine woman so that I can care for those that are sick and those that are injured. I have to care for Fox until he no longer needs me or my medicines."

"Mother," Fawn scowled and the frown creased her mouth. "How can you care for someone when you are falling asleep standing up? Let someone else care for him."

"I agree," Gesher added as he poked his mate. "Now that Marmot is here, she can take care of him while you, and I, get some rest."

Marmot glanced up from where she was sitting while she cradled Fox's head on her lap. "Of course I can give him the medicine. Just tell me what to give him and how to give it to him."

Ibex looked at Marmot, then at Gesher and finally to Fawn and Lynx. "You are right, I do need sleep as does Gesher. We have not slept since Fox was hurt. Here is the pain medicine. If he starts to moan or thrash around give this to him. This is the sleeping medicine. Give it to him just as the Sun Spirit starts to sink below the horizon." She stretched and shrugged her shoulders to loosen them up. "But wake me and Gesher if you think there is anything wrong or if he seems to be getting worse."

Fawn touched her mother on the shoulder. "Go and get some sleep. Lynx and I will stay with Marmot and help her if she needs any help caring for Fox."

"But he needs a medicine woman, and I am the only medicine woman of The Chosen here."

"No you are not!" Fawn told her as she sat down by Fox and Marmot. "I am a medicine woman of The Chosen. I have watched you; you have explained the plants and how they are used many times to me. I have sat next to you and saw how the medicines are made and how to give them to people. I did not come out of your belly, but I am your daughter and I know how to care for people and what medicines to use."

Ibex shook her head up and down. "Of course you are. I am so sleepy that I was not thinking. It is good that you can care for people as a medicine woman of The Chosen."

Gesher nodded and a smile slowly spread across his face. "My daughter speaks the truth. Ibex did not birth you; we found you buried in a pile of boulders and almost dead when you were still a little baby. But you are my daughter in my heart. I love you as much as any man can love a baby born to his mate."

Fawn reached out and tugged at the man's leg. "I love you too, if anyone ever told me that I was not loved by the man I call Dada, I would know that they were not saying what is true."

Gesher bent down and took her face in his hands. "You are loved more than you will ever know. You are the daughter that did not come out of Ibex's belly."

Fawn took his hands in hers as she rose to her feet. Wrapping her arms around the waist of the tall, pale skinned man, she tilted her head upward and kissed him. "I love you, Dada."

"I love you!" He answered softly as his hand tenderly caressed her face. "The spirits brought me a daughter, a daughter who is very precious to me. I am blessed by the spirits with a mate that I love and who loves me. A son who did come out of Ibex's belly and is loved, and you."

"Go and get some sleep, Lynx and I can take care of what is needed. I worry about you and my Mama. I love the two of you and worry about you."

"Don't worry about us, you have a son and he needs your worry. He is a baby and needs attention all the time. You and Lynx must care for him as you and he were cared for."

"He is, and we do," Fawn replied touching Gesher tenderly on the cheek. "I have enough love for him, for Lynx, for you and my mother. I am a woman of The Chosen. I can do many things at the same time."

"Gesher, come with me," Ibex said, as she took him by the hand. "Fawn and Lynx can care for Fox. We need to sleep."

Boar walked over to where Fox lay on the ground. He sent a series of signs to Snake and Hawk telling them to come where he was and to join the people gathered around Fox. "Our clan has a custom," he said softly to Fawn. "The custom is that we gather close to someone who is sick or hurt and pray to the spirits for help. If you do not want us to ask for the help of the spirits, we will not. But I have learned much from Gesher and Ibex and I want to be shown more. Your clan is like the clans of The Chosen, yet you are not. I can't explain what or why but the differences make your clan, the Clan of Ibex, different from us."

"You can, what was the word you said? I think it was pray? We also sit by the person who is sick or injured and ask the spirits for help in making the person better. We will all sit by Fox and ask for, or as you say, pray for, Fox."

The Sun Spirit was waking in the east when Boar and his two hunters stood. "We are going," he said quietly. "But as we leave know this. My clan and I will welcome you if you decide to visit. The Clan of Ibex has found friends and a clan that wants to trade and learn more about them and these other people called The Second People."

"Thank you Boar, as the daughter of Ibex and Gesher, the leaders of our clan, I take your hand in friendship. Go with the spirits and our friendship. Be safe in what you do."

"You and your clan also go with the spirits," Boar replied giving her hand a squeeze. Be safe in what you do and keep the spirits with you as you travel."

A moan from Fox made the conversation cease and they looked at him.

"It is time for more medicine," Lynx said reaching for the piles of medicinal plants that were arranged close to the place where Fox lay. "Do you want the medicine that is for pain, or the medicine that is for sleep?"

Fawn dropped down to her knees and felt Fox's forehead. Then she probed the places under his chin, the left armpit, the groin region and other places known to the medicine women of The Chosen as the areas where signs of illness in a person were hidden. "No," she said shaking her head from side to side. "No more medicines to make him sleep. It is time to let him wake and as a man of The Chosen learn to live with the pain."

"But," Lynx started to say when he heard Ibex's voice.

"Has the fever gone?"

Fawn glanced up and smiled. "The fever is gone and the secret places in a person's body, where we look for and find signs of illness, are not swollen."

"If he has no fever and there are no lumps in the places where a person who is sick has lumps, then you are right. It is time to stop giving him medicine and let him wake. He is a man of The Chosen and will endure the pain."

Boar looked at Ibex and Fawn. "You both are well trained in the secrets of medicine women. The Clan of Ibex is fortunate to have two who are skilled in the powers of the plants."

"Gesher thinks that this clan is special to the spirits. He has said that we are a clan of The Chosen, but also of The Second People. Gesher, Wolf and Rabbit are of The Second People. Ibex, Marmot and Fox are of The Chosen as am I," Fawn said softly. Lynx is different, his Dada is of The Second People but his Mama is of The Chosen. We are both, but prefer to be clan."

"Then as a clan of The Chosen, you should come to the gathering," Boar said as he started down the trail.

Ibex's head jerked up at the word gathering. "There is a gathering of clans? Where is the gathering?"

"Hawk stopped and then walked back. Dropping down on the ground, he pushed the stones and sticks out of the way until he had a clear space. Then he poked at the dirt with his finger. You go this way; you said you call it west, for three mountain ridges. When you come to a large river that is in the valley after climbing down from the third mountain you turn," he paused as he tried to think, "You turn north!" He exclaimed loudly with a grin spreading across his face as he remembered the word. "Travel north following the river for five days, perhaps six days. The clan gathering is where the two large rivers meet. It is also the home of the Dordogne Clan.
We will be there, as will the Moula Clan. Will the Clan of Ibex come and join the gathering?"

Boar waited patiently as Hawk drew the way on the dirt. "Yes, it would be good for you to come. I would like to see the other clans' look on their faces when your clan arrives. But," he added as he thought about the way he had acted when he first saw Gesher, "we will send runners ahead to tell the other clans that there is a stranger coming whose skin is almost so thin that you can see the blood under it. But that he is a good and trusted friend of The Chosen."

"When is the Gathering?" Ibex asked as she watched Fox.

"Fall, we are planning on gathering in the fall when the leaves start to fall from the trees and the face on the moon is full."

6

We have been walking for five days," Marmot said as she glanced at Fox. "Should someone go on ahead and see how much further it is? Fox is tired."

"No I'm not," Fox answered as he adjusted the pack slightly that was tied to his back. "It's just that this pack is rubbing my back raw and I need to stop and tie it differently."

"Well, I could use some rest," Fawn said, as she stopped and put Badger down. Rabbit put Ox down, and the two young boys immediately began to crawl toward each other. "I think Ox wants to play with Badger," Wolf said watching his son slowly move over the rough ground.

Ibex's quick fleeting look at the two mothers helped her to make up her mind. "We will stop here and rest for many heartbeats, then look for a place to stop and make camp for the night. Hawk had said five or six days walking when he told us where to go."

"Hunters can move a lot faster than families with children," Gesher said as he shrugged his shoulders letting the packs slip off. "Even carrying loads of meat, a hunter can travel further in a day than a mother with a child."

Fox sat down and let Marmot rub his red sore shoulder. "There has to be a better way to tie the pack so that I can walk with it and it does not move on my shoulder."

Marmot's hands massaged his shoulder then sent a silent sign to Ibex. "Is there something you can put on his shoulder? It is very raw."

Gesher saw the signal and meandered over to where Fox and Marmot were sitting. "Fox, your shoulder looks as red as my skin does if I am out in the sun for a long time. How does it feel?"

"It hurts, but it is nothing that I can't endure. The pain in my right shoulder, where the arm used to be, was much worse when I woke up after Ibex cut it off. Even after a moon, the pain was worse than it is now."

"I have an idea," Gesher said taking a large piece of hide from his traveling pack. "Lets try folding this skin and putting it under the strap so that the strap rubs the hide and not your left shoulder."

"It is a good idea!"

"Is everyone rested enough to continue the walk?" Ibex asked as she rose to her feet, "or should we stay a few heartbeats longer?"

"We are ready to go," Fawn said, picking Badger up and cradling him to her breast.

"So are we," Wolf answered as he picked up Ox.

"If they are ready so are we," Fox said to Ibex.

"If I remember what we were told, we must be getting close," Gesher said, as they turned a corner in the trail. "This is the sixth day of walking since we turned north."

"There is a foot print!" Fox exclaimed, as he bent down to look at the scuffmark in the grass.

"And a broken twig," Marmot added looking at the jagged edge of the branch. "And I see more sign, it looks like a large group came down the trail from that direction," she pointed, "and now they are traveling in front of us."

Ibex nodded her head in agreement. "Watch for the signs that will tell us how long ago they made the tracks and left the signs."

"They made a fire here. Perhaps it was a camp where they stayed overnight, or maybe just stopped and made a fire to heat some meat." Lynx said as he reached into the ashes. "I can still feel some heat in the ashes. If the ash still has heat, then they did not leave here a long time ago."

"Here is some dung," Gesher said from the edge of the trail. "It is not animal dung, and I can feel heat in it. They are not that far ahead of us."

Ibex and Fawn squatted on the trail and inhaled the scent of the dung. Then Marmot picked up a small amount of dung and tasted it. "Fresh," Marmot said as she spit the dung out. "They are very close, we could catch up to them if we hurry."

"Then we will hurry," Fox said as he again took up the trail.

The Sun Spirit began to sink lower in the west as Fox and Marmot crested a knoll and looked over the side of the hill.

"There, look there!" Marmot exclaimed as she pointed down to a place where the trail twisted through the thick forest of pine and hardwood. "There is someone."

"Yes," Fox said as he quickened his pace, then turned back to yell at those trailing behind them. "We see people on the trail."

The sighting of people ahead of them on the trail made the whole group increase the speed of their walking. It was not quite running, but it was much faster than walking.

"Do you hear that?" Rabbit asked as she tilted her head slightly to the side.

"What?" Gesher asked as he tried to hear what Rabbit said she heard. "Did it sound like danger?"

"No, it sounds like a lot of people talking."

"Look!" Fox said holding up his hand. "I see smoke from campfires, many campfires."

"Then we are at the gathering," Ibex said, breaking into a run. "Hurry, so we get there before the Sun Spirit goes to sleep."

As they approached the site of the gathering, the voices slowly ended their conversations as everyone looked at the group coming toward them.

"There they are," a familiar voice boomed out from the hushed assembled clans. "I told you that they would come. And," he said, even louder, "did I not say that they were a clan of The Chosen that was not like any assembled here."

"It has to be a spirit," another voice answered.

"No he is not a spirit. His name is Gesher, and he lives and breathes as we do," the familiar voice responded.

"It seems that Boar is having problems convincing the people here that we are clan, and that you, my mate, are not a spirit," Ibex said, as she told her clan to stop where they were.

"Boar," she called out, "how are you? We have come to the gathering as you suggested. We have much to trade."

"Who is that female calling out to you?" Another voice asked. "Why would the leader allow a woman to speak to the leader of another clan?"

"Because," Boar replied quietly, sending a signal to Ibex to come and join him. "That woman you are talking about is Ibex, and she is the leader of the Clan of Ibex."

"Then they are not clan," the man snarled, and started to walk away from Boar.

"I tell you that not only are they clan, but a new clan, a clan that did not exist before. Ibex and her mate Gesher, the man with the skin so white it looks like the milk seeping from a new mother's breast, are the first two people of a new clan that now numbers eight. They have grown and prospered for many springs."

"Then where is their cave, where do they call home?"

"Gesher says that they are still searching for someplace that is right for them. But that he, and the man called Wolf, and the woman called Rabbit, are not of The Chosen by birth. They became members of the Clan of Ibex by choice. That they are from a people that are called The Second People." Boar paused and looked at the man standing there. "They like to wander and to find new valleys and mountains to hunt and to live. They are coming into our valleys and our mountains."

"They will be welcomed to visit and to trade, if that is what they want, but these valleys, these hills, these rivers and these mountains are where we have lived for as long as we have memories. They can't stay, this is the home of The Chosen!"

Boar nodded and motioned to Ibex as he said to her and her clan, "Come and meet the leader of the clan known as The Dordogne. He is called Rhino."

Ibex approached the man and took his hand in her two hands then squeezed, "I am happy to meet you Rhino of The Dordogne. My clan and I have much to trade and we are always looking for new friends. This is my mate. His name is Gesher."

"Welcome to the home of The Dordogne. You know Boar; he is the leader of the Clan of Chapelle. The Moula Clan is already here and camped further up the river. The leader of The Moula is named Deer. He is the one who said that the Neander Clan is also going to be here."

"The Neander Clan?" Ibex asked and her voice almost sounded as if it was a sigh mixed with a whisper. "If they are coming, it would be a great honor to Rhino and his clan."

"That is what we have been told. A runner was sent last spring saying they wanted to come to the next gathering, wherever it was going to be. That they had something to say, something to tell the clans."

"What?" Gesher asked, looking first at Boar and then at Rhino. "Did the runner say what the Neander Clan wanted to tell the clans? Have you heard what it is that they want to tell us?"

Rhino looked at Gesher and frowned. "This is talk between leaders. You are only the mate of a leader. Stay if you want, but only listen."

Ibex glared at Rhino. "He is more than my mate. Gesher is also a leader of the Clan of Ibex. We have two leaders."

Rhino looked at Boar and his face almost, but not completely, changed expression. "Two leaders for one clan. That is not the way of The Chosen."

Boar just smiled and shrugged his shoulders. "You have been warned, Rhino. These people, this Clan of Ibex, are a new clan. They think differently, they do things not as we have always done it, and they seek new ideas."

"Who are these people?" A voice boomed across the opening. "Why was I not told another clan had come?"

Boar turned and waved. "Deer it is good of you to come. This is Ibex from the Clan of Ibex. Ibex this is Deer of the Dordogne Clan."

Ibex grasped the hand of Deer between her two hands and squeezed. "I am happy to meet you Deer, leader of the Dordogne

100

Clan. This man here is my mate, and also a leader of the Clan of Ibex. His name is Gesher."

"The Clan of Ibex? I never heard of a clan that was called Ibex. Where do you come from?"

Ibex gave his hand another squeeze and pointed first to the east, then to the north, and finally to the south. "We come from all places, and all clans. We have no cave to call our home, no mountain to call our own. We travel and seek new friends and people to trade with."

Deer tried to keep from staring at Gesher, but even with his head turned toward Ibex, his eyes still glanced every few heartbeats toward the tall pale man. "Ibex," he said slowly, as he turned toward Gesher. "Your mate is certainly tall, I have never seen a man that was so tall. My head seems to only come up to his shoulder."

"He is probably even taller," Ibex replied with a slight laugh to her voice. "He is tall even for the people that he left to seek a great adventure. That is how he found me, and I found him. We were both alone and stumbled into each other."

Boar looked at Gesher and then at Ibex. "You both were alone? That is a tale that has to be told around a campfire late at night. I want to hear how a woman of The Chosen was alone."

"Patience Boar," Deer told him. "That is a tale we all will hear tonight as we gather to talk and tell tales of our clans. But I must know more about Gesher. He can talk can't he? Or did whatever it was that made his skin so pale also make him unable to talk?"

"I can talk as well as you can. And my hand signs and signals are better than most," Gesher answered, and saw the look on the man's face. "I was born this way. The man who was the mate of my mother also looked this way. I am unusual but not strange. I am just different."

"And he is an experienced healer," Ibex added, as she reached out took his hand. "In the far away places he called home, those who are knowledgeable in the ways of the medicine plants are called healers. He traveled far, and was alone for many springs before I found him. I will tell that tale tonight at the campfires. But perhaps he should be the one to tell it."

"Whoever tells the tale, the whole camp will be listening. I would think that no tale from any clan will be better than the tales that we will hear from the Clan of Ibex."

Ibex waited a heartbeat waiting for either Deer or Rhino to speak, then turned back toward where the rest of her clan stood. "We will make camp up on that knoll, near where the three large pines are bending toward each other and touching each other. That will keep us close to the water but away from the direct light from the Sun Spirit. That way Gesher will be protected from the burning Sun Spirit and his skin will not blister and peel when we are asked to be the clan to host the meals for one day. He can sit in the shade and talk to all who come by to trade or just find out more about us. It seems that we are the talk of the gathering, at least until the Neander Clan gets here with the news that they are bringing."

Fox stood there for a few heartbeats looking at the three sites already claimed by the three clans that were there. "They are all along the river, we will be the only clan that is in the shade of the tall trees." He paused for only a heartbeat before smiling and saying just loud enough to be heard by those people from the other clans who were close by, "Ibex picked the best place for our clan. Just close enough to the river so we do not have to walk far, but hidden in the shade of the pines and hardwoods so we have cover."

Gesher paused and quickly walked after Rhino. "There are many people here, and when the Neander clan comes there will be more. Have you hidden meat that I do not see?"

"No, my pale-skinned friend. But I have planned a massive hunt. There is a large valley just over that ridge, and we have not hunted there since spring. The valley has many horses, deer, ox and if we are blessed by the spirits, maybe bison and elephants. The last hunt was not a hunt to hunt, it was a scouting hunt."

"When is this hunt?"

"We will hunt in two days. Every man and woman will go. The only ones who will stay behind are those with small children, the children of course, and those like Fox who can't hunt."

"Fox can hunt!" Gesher said, and whistled to get the attention of his clan. "Fox come here."

"Fox, if we went hunting in two days would you stay and watch the babies and the children while we hunted?" Gesher asked, and then winked at the young man.

Fox saw the wink and realized that this was a test. "Am I not a man?" He shouted, banging the butt of his spear on the ground to show his pretended unhappiness. "Am I an old man who must be cared for like a newborn baby? I am Fox, a man of the Clan of Ibex. I am a hunter."

Rhino looked at the young man and shook his head. "But can you hunt like a hunter? Can you carry a spear and throw it? If another hunter was in danger could you assist him? I will not endanger anyone on a hunt just to take someone along who is not able to take care of himself."

Fox's face started to turn the color of the Sun Spirit when he was high overhead on a clear cloudless day. "Not only can I take care of myself, I still hunt and contribute to the food supply of my clan. A spear is thrown with just one arm."

"But can you have a second spear ready in the other hand, or a club? What about skinning or butchering?"

"What about skinning or butchering?" Fox replied, glaring at the man. "An animal is hung from a stout limb for butchering. As for skinning an animal, I have not had any problems with the deer or horses I have killed. In the Clan of Ibex, we cooperate and help each other."

Gesher stood there trying not to smile. At first it was just a joke, and Fox had realized that Gesher was trying to fool Rhino, but then Rhino had actually provoked Fox by what he had said. Fox was actually angry.

Ibex walked over and tried to get in-between Fox and Rhino but the two men were almost bumping chests. "Fox," she cautioned, forcing her self between them. "Rhino and his clan are the host clan for the gathering. It is not right to argue with him."

"He has insulted me," Fox shouted. "No man insults another unless he wants to provoke that man."

Rhino looked at Ibex and then at Gesher, and finally at the number of people from all the clans that were milling around where he and Fox were standing. In the clans of The Chosen, actually provoking another man was serious. Provoking a man could cause a fight, a fight could cause an injury and an injury could cause death. The potential of a death or even injury to a man had the potential of causing serious harm to the clan. The loss of a hunter would impact the ability of the clan to provide enough meat to last through the long cold moons that lasted from fall to spring. It could mean the difference between surviving or not surviving for the whole clan.

Rhino held up his hands, palm up and fingers extended. It was an easily recognized sign that all knew. "I am sorry," he said slowly but loudly enough to be heard by everyone gathered around them. "What I was saying was not meant to provoke Fox. He is a brave man to have had his right arm amputated. I have not questioned his honor or his ability. I was just asking a question that was misunderstood. For that I apologize to Fox and his clan. When we go on the hunt he can go with me and protect my back while I protect his. I will put my life in his hands."

The bright red color of pent up anger slowly drained from Fox's face and even Gesher let a deep sigh escape from his chest. For a man to say that he was willing to put his life in the hands of another man was important. It was the ultimate apology.

"They are coming," the shout was picked up and repeated as more people saw the clan round the top of the hill and start down the trail. "The Neander Clan is here."

The Neander Clan slowly meandered along the trail toward the place were the gathering was located. The exhaustion was evident, even on the faces of the strongest males in the clan. They had been traveling for nearly a full moon to reach the place of the gathering. As they drew near, people raced out to greet them and took much of the load off their shoulders as they grabbed packs and bundles.

Rhino grasped the hand of Mammoth and squeezed. "You must be very tired. Pick a campsite and have your people rest and recover from the long journey. When the Sun Spirit wakes in the morning, we will talk about what it is that you want to tell all of us. Then the next day, we have planned a massive hunt. If you and your hunters are still tired, you can stay in the camp. Or, if you are not too tired, you can join the hunt. But enough of my talking, seek your resting place and sleep."

Mammoth withdrew his hand and resumed the trek toward the place where his experience told him was the best place to have his people put up their shelters. "Many of my people are nearly exhausted. The traveling was hard and the distance great. But before I seek a place to sleep for the night, hear what I say."

"Shouldn't it wait until all the leaders of the clans have assembled?" Rhino asked, as he looked out to where Ibex and her people were sitting around their fires, and then to where Boar and his people sat enjoying their night meal. "We have five clans here for the gathering. Never have there been five at one gathering."

"Better five than just two," Mammoth replied. "I will tell more at the assembly of leaders. But listen well old friend. The snows are coming earlier and staying later. Fall begins early and spring seems to never come." He paused as he pulled at his beard. "And the mammoth and the reindeer, along with the Woolly Rhino, are moving toward you and out of our valleys."

"But they have been in your valleys for as long as the Neander Clan has been in the mountains," Rhino said, with a look on his face that seemed to be one of disbelief. "Have you and your hunters been hunting them too hard?"

"No, in fact we have been trying to not hunt them. But slowly they are leaving and coming down the rivers towards where your clans stay. We saw a herd of perhaps 20 mammoths just three days journey from here. They were moving along the valley floor and heading this way."

"The assembly of leaders must hear this," Rhino responded to the statement. "Perhaps the medicine women and those that speak to the spirits should also come to the assembly."

"Perhaps, but right now all I want to do is get some sleep."

7

The Sun Spirit finally broke the horizon and began to cause long shadows on the ground. But the rising sun and lengthening shadows did not find the clans sleeping. The hunters were already packed and starting down the trail. The rest of the people were preparing the site for their return. Fire pits were being deepened and more rocks piled around the edges. More firewood was being piled near the fire pits. Skinning blades were being examined while the skilled toolmakers sat making more. The very elderly tried to keep the young children from interfering too much with the preparations for the coming feast and celebration when the hunters returned. It had been a long discussion between the clan leaders as to where to hunt and what to hunt.

Ibex and Gesher, along with Mammoth, had talked about hunting the mammoths that were - at least were a few days ago - moving toward them. Rhino and Deer had argued for concentrating on the large herds of ox and bison that were everywhere. It was Boar who helped make up their minds. "Why not just let the spirits decide? What we hunt will be what they want us to hunt. If we see mammoth we will hunt mammoth. If a large herd of bison is seen, we will hunt bison. We have always trusted in the spirits to lead us. Why not trust them to show us what it is that they want us to hunt?"

The Sun Spirit was at the tips of the tallest trees when the two hunters that were the scouts signaled a halt. Signs and signals flew between the scouts and the clan leaders. Treading softly on the leaves and pine boughs, the scouts worked their way back to the main hunting party. "The valley ahead is full of animals. There are deer, bison, ox, horses and mammoth."

Ibex tapped Rhino on the arm, "Mammoth, we should hunt the mammoth. Three or four mammoth would be the same as 15 or 20 bison. Five mammoths would feed all the clans until spring. That would be one mammoth for each clan."

Rhino shook his head. "Mammoth are large and dangerous. Only Mammoth himself and his hunters have ever hunted mammoth."

"No, that is not true. I have hunted elephant and so has Gesher and Fox and Rabbit. Where Gesher used to live, there are elephants. They are like mammoths, but they do not have the long hair that mammoth have. Where elephants live, the days are warm and there is no snow. We carry spears that were first made long ago by a female hunter named Caraga. She thought of the blade. Have you not realized that the spears carried by the men and women of the Clan of Ibex are not like yours?"

"It has been seen, but we did not want to say anything. We did not want to offend you by saying your tool makers were not skilled enough to make better points."

"We can make thinner points, but they would not be better. These spears have killed the terrible one, a megaloceros and many other large animals. They are made the way they look because they are able to penetrate deep and cut a wide path."

"You killed one of the terrible ones? How many in your clan were killed?"

"None! And when we faced three of them, killing the one who attacked, there were just four of us in the clan and Fawn was still not yet a grown woman. But she drove her spear into the terrible one. Her killing scream was heard by the other two females and they slunk away into the forest."

"What about the megaloceros? Who killed it?"

"It was Fawn who was the hunt leader. She tracked it and made the plan for the attack. It was her spear, and the spear of Lynx her mate, that drew first blood."

Glancing at Fawn, he smiled and then winked as he tilted his head slightly. "I wish that she was my mate. She is a woman!"

"But she is not, she is my woman!" Lynx said, with barely controlled anger showing in his voice.

"Enough of this," Mammoth said, as he tried to regain control of the hunt. "Have all the leaders agreed on hunting the mammoth?"

"Yes!" they nearly all said in unison.

Ibex looked at Gesher, then sent him a quick flurry of signs but limited them to the type of signs that just used the fingers or a very slight movement of the hand. When she saw him nod his head in agreement, she winked at him, and then whistled shrilly. Her whistle sounded almost exactly like the cry of a hunting hawk.

The whistle caused nearly every head to turn toward her. Her hands flew as she got the attention of all of the leaders. Her whisper was just loud enough for those standing within two or three paces to hear her words. The others that were further away watched her hands and fingers as she sent them her message.

"Listen to what I have to say," Ibex signed and said quietly. "Our hunters carry the spears that are used by the people where Gesher, Wolf and Rabbit come from. The first blade was made by a female hunter who was called Caraga. Since then, all the hunters who call themselves members of The Second People carry this type of spear. It is broader and larger, yet it is thinner. It penetrates deep and cuts a large path." She paused as she held her spear up and slowly turned it so that all could see the shaft of the spear and the finely honed blade that was attached to it. "It is the best spear to kill the mammoth. We have extra spears that we would give as gifts to the other clans. All we need are two spears for each hunter. The other two that we carry are for anyone who wants to use the spears that The Second People call the elephant killers."

Wolf looked at Rabbit then leaned over and whispered very quietly in her ear. The whisper was so soft and muffled that even Marmot,

109

who was standing less than a pace away did not hear the words. "I never heard the word elephant killer used to tell of our spear points. Is Ibex saying something that I have no knowledge of?"

Rabbit smiled and then kissed her mate. "I think I know," she whispered back, as her lips brushed his ear. "She is making a tale to make sure that they all know the power of our blades."

"Oh," he mumbled, then turned back and watched the expressions on the faces of the hunters from the other clans.

Mammoth, the leader of the Neander Clan just stood there. "What did she just do? Did she bite her mate?" His signal was brief but the look on his face and the faces of the others gathered around the Clan of Ibex were unimaginable.

Ibex glanced over at Wolf and Rabbit and shook her head. "They just kissed, that is all. It is a way for two people who are mates to say that the other is special and that they are loved."

"Loved?"

"I will explain more about kissing, and about what love is, at the fires after we kill the mammoth. But now we should think about the best way to stalk and kill the mammoth. Who wants to carry one of our special spears?"

The extra spears were soon distributed among the other clans and the leaders began to talk of the hunting strategy.

"Then it is agreed," Mammoth said, as he stood and sent a signal to his hunters. "Each clan will pick one mammoth and only one. We will wait for the signals that each clan is in place and then attack all at once. This plan is a good one. If each clan does as the leader has said, we will all have mammoth meat for winter."

Ibex sent a fast sign to her hunters and then crouched low and started to run toward the east. Fox and Marmot were right behind her, as were the other hunters of her clan.

"There is the one we are hunting," Ibex signaled as she stopped and pointed toward the slowly moving herd of mammoth. "The large cow with the torn ear. I picked that one."

"It is the matriarch, the leader of the herd," Gesher said, as he saw where her spear was pointing. "The meat will be tough."

"Yes, the meat will need to be chewed and chewed. But the hide is large and the honor of killing such an animal is important. I picked this animal for four reasons. One, it is the matriarch and when she falls the herd will have no leader. Two, she is the biggest and when our spears kill her it will prove that our spears and the blades that we use, are the best. Three, some of these people are still unsure of a woman being a hunter. None of the other clans that are here have females in the hunting party. And four, I have to prove to a few of them that I can be a leader of a clan."

"Why?" Marmot asked, as she stood there watching the herd.

"It is the tradition of The Chosen to have males as leaders. Remember that our clan is different from any clan of The Chosen or from any band of The Second People. In the Clan of Ibex we have traditions from both. Gesher and I talked and talked about which ones we would use."

Gesher nodded. "We, the Clan of Ibex, have both ways. If we thought that The Chosen way was best, then we followed the ways of The Chosen. If we thought that the ways of The Second People were best, we followed that way. We are the only people that follow the ways of two people. We are the first!"

"Enough talking," Ibex whispered. "It is time to think of the stalk and the kill. Gesher you take the lead. We have to circle the herd. The position for our attack on the herd is from the east. When we are ready I will signal. The other leaders will signal when they are in position. After all clans are in position, and Mammoth thinks everything is ready, he will send another signal and we all will attack the mammoth we have selected. The attack will be all at the same heartbeat, or at least as close to it as we can be."

Ibex dropped to her knees and began to crawl even closer. As she edged closer and closer to the massive mammoth, she sent her signal to the other leaders. But even after the signal had been sent she continued to signal her hunters forward.

As the other clans moved into the positions that their leaders wanted, more signals were heard. Mammoth listened intently for the series of signals that would mean all the clans were exactly where they should have been. As the last signal, the one from the Moula Clan was heard, he sniffed the air. Then he tasted the air. His ears and eyes focused intently on the herd as it fed. His shrill signal pierced the still air. All around the herd the men, and a few women, rose to their feet and threw their spears.

The mammoth herd raised their trunks and trumpeted warnings to each other. The large leader of the herd, the oldest and wisest of all the females in the herd, blasted her warning to the other females and young in her herd. But her cry was cut short as the spears from Ibex and her clan thudded into her body. Gesher's spear pierced the tough leathery hide just behind the right front leg. Fox's spear hit barely a hand's width to the left of Gesher's spear. Both spears were buried in the pachyderm's heart. Fawn's spear, along with the spear of Lynx, slid between the protective ribs and sliced into the lungs. Those four spears were more than enough to kill even the largest and strongest animal, but the remaining spears were also well within the chest area. All the spears had been thrown within two heartbeats of hearing the signal.

The matriarch of the mammoth herd tried to attack her tormentors. Her muscular trunk stretched toward where the Clan of Ibex stood and she lurched forward. "Save your spears," Ibex shouted, as she saw her hunters shifting their second spears into throwing position. "She is already falling, see the way her legs are shaking."

Before the last word had been shouted, the leader of the herd stumbled as her legs gave way and she crashed to the ground. "She

112

is down, she will never rise again. Concentrate on another animal. See that young bull racing for the cover of the trees? The distance is far; we will have to aim far above his back to adjust for the fall of our spears. Remember to aim way above the back and in front of him so the spears will hit in the right place to kill him. I do not want to be tracking a wounded mammoth in the forest. Take aim and throw now!"

Her spear was the first to fly toward the running young bull. It arched high in the air, nearly twice the height of the bull's broad back and well in front of where he was as the spear was thrown. The rest of the clan's spears were right behind hers. Eight spears arched high in the air then began to fall downward. For a few heartbeats, Ibex and her hunters watched the spears and the young bull race toward each other.

Fox was holding his breath without even knowing he was holding it. As the first spear drove into the bull's hide he yelped and then inhaled. In less than one heartbeat all the spears were slicing into the chest region of the bull.

"It looks good," Gesher yelled, and began running toward the staggering bull. "I think that they are all well within the killing area. We will have much to brag about at the campfires tonight. Two mammoths killed for the Clan of Ibex."

"Wait," Lynx shouted as he bent over the cow and pulled out a spear. "Have you forgotten what it was that you taught us? Never be without a spear! A man without a spear is a dead man walking."

"Throw me a spear,"

"Here, take this one," Lynx said as he handed a spear to Gesher. "I will take this one. Fox, grab a spear and join us. We are going to make sure the bull is dead."

"Be careful," Rabbit shouted, as she bent over and began to gut the huge matriarch.

"Pull on that side of the hide," Ibex said, as she struggled to cut out the intestines from the mammoth. "I want the heart, liver and kidneys. That will be more than enough for our feast tonight as we celebrate the hunt."

"The tongue, I think the tongue is one of the best tasting pieces of any animal that is large enough to use the skin for clothing. Cut out the tongue." Fawn asked, as she pulled as hard as she could on the flap of hide where Ibex was cutting into the guts. "Tongue is as good as liver or heart when it is eaten right after a kill."

Lynx approached the mammoth silently while watching the eyes. Beside him Gesher and Wolf kept their spears poised for a quick throw. "He just blinked," Gesher shouted. "Watch out! He is still alive."

The young bull, nearly at the age where the matriarch and the other females of the herd would have forced him to leave, rolled his eyes and looked at the three hunters coming ever closer. His trunk snaked out as he tried to grasp one of them with it.

Gesher pulled back his arm as he readied his spear. His fingers felt for the perfect balance and he bounced it slightly to adjust the position where he was holding it.

"Wait," Fox shouted, "hold your spear, don't throw it yet. There is a wounded mammoth coming right at us!"

Lynx and Gesher turned at the shout and saw a large female running right at them. Her trumpet, as she neared the three hunters, was a combination of the pain she was feeling from the spears imbedded in her side and anger toward the puny animals that were standing in her way. Behind the female, racing as fast as they could, were the hunters from the Dordogne Clan. "Watch out," Rhino shouted, as he paused to catch his breath.

At the site where Ibex and the others from her clan were slowly skinning and butchering their kill, the shouted warning made all of them pause and look up. "That mammoth is heading right for Gesher, Lynx and Fox," Ibex screamed. "Grab any spear you can and come with me. We have to try to get there before the wounded cow does."

"It can't be done," Fawn cried. "The distance is too far. She will be upon them before we, or anyone from the Dordogne Clan can get close enough to help."

"We have to try!" Ibex yelled as she grabbed a spear and began to run. "Come with me, or stay and skin the old cow, but I am going to try to save my mate and my son."

"Spread out," Gesher said calmly, as he watched the wounded cow come closer and closer. "No, even further. Make sure the distance between us is more than she can reach without twisting around."

"Steady, watch for the killing area to show. A spear in the ear or trunk is a wasted throw. Do not throw when she is flapping her ears or has her trunk toward the ground. Aim for the chest where it meets the neck as soon as her trunk is raised and her ears are back. Wait for my signal, and then throw for the place where the neck and chest are connected. Ready, now!"

Three spears hurtled from three separate directions but all three reached the same place at the same heartbeat. The sharp broad yet thin blades of the elephant killing spears penetrated deep into the chest wall. One actually sliced completely through the windpipe of the charging mammoth. She tried to trumpet her distress but couldn't even make a sound. Soundlessly, she crumpled to the ground, kicked three times and lay there.

"Her eyes are open and she is not breathing," Fox said, as he reached for his spear.

"Fox, that was a lucky throw," Lynx said, as he saw where the spear thrown by Fox had hit. "Your spear cut her windpipe. She couldn't breathe with her windpipe cut in two."

Rhino stood there looking at Fox and where his thrown spear had been thrown. "If it was not a lucky throw, it must have been thrown by one of the best hunters that The Chosen have in any clan."

Gesher looked at Rhino and then at Fox. "Perhaps the spirits were watching where the spear was to go. Or," he added softly and his arm embraced Fox, "this man, even with one arm, is as good a hunter as most men with both arms. And braver than most."

Lynx nodded, then turned back toward the young bull that now lay dead on the grass behind them. "We have a mammoth to gut, skin and butcher. You had better start on this one."

"This is your kill," Rhino said quietly. "It is your spears that killed it. Our spears only wounded it. The meat and hide belong to the Clan of Ibex."

"No, the kill is yours," Ibex answered as she arrived at the kill. "You drew first blood."

"A wounded animal is not a kill."

"That is true, but I see where your spears are, or were before they fell out. The mammoth would have died from its wounds. All my hunters did was finish the hunt for you. The kill is yours. We have two mammoths and that is enough for any clan." Ibex signaled her hunters and they left Rhino and his hunters with the dead cow.

"I have been wrong," Rhino yelled after Ibex, as he watched Ibex and her hunters leave. "You have made me see that I was wrong. A woman can be a leader of a clan. You are really a leader that The Chosen can learn from. I look forward to talking to you and your people around the campfires. What you have to trade will be welcomed at the campfire of the Dordogne Clan."

Ibex signaled her hunters as they drew near the second kill, the young bull. "Gesher, pick three hunters to help you gut, skin and butcher this kill. The rest of us will go back to the old cow and finish gutting, skinning and butchering her. As soon as one of the mammoths is finished, the ones who are done will come and help the ones still working. There is a lot of food here. Two mammoths will feed our clan for many moons."

Lynx nodded as he looked over the two carcasses of the slain mammoths. "There is so much here that some of it will spoil and become rotten before we can eat it all. I would not want to make the spirits mad by wasting meat from the animals that they have sent us."

"It is not good to make the spirits angry," Fox agreed as he bent over the kill and started to peel the thick hairy coat of hair off the mammoth. "But what can we do? They sent the herd to us. We killed two of them, and helped kill a third. We only did what hunters have done since we were pulled from the ground by the spirits.

"What if," Fawn asked looking at Ibex, "we gave some of the meat to the other clans? We share what we have killed with each other. Any kill is shared with the other families in our clan. Why not share with all the families in all the clans?"

Marmot glanced up from where she sat, carefully peeling the skin off the mammoth. "Sharing with the others is a good idea. I think we should share what meat we do not need for the winter with the other clans. When Fox was injured and still not able to hunt, we lived on the food that was shared with us. I know that is the way of The Chosen and also The Second People."

She paused and drew in a large lungful of air before saying any more. "But, I can look at our clan and see more than The Chosen or The Second People. I see in our clan the ways of The Chosen and the ways of The Second People. We use words from both, we use traditions of both, we tell tales of the beginning when we first were pulled from the ground by the spirits. We have made up words and signs that have never been used by anyone. New words and signs that we now use that were never said by The Chosen or

The Second People. New hand signs and signals that were never used by The Second People or by The Chosen."

Fox shook his head and took his mate by the hands. "I hear your words but do not understand what you are saying."

"I think I do," Gesher said, "but tell us more of what you are thinking."

Marmot looked at the co-leader of their clan. The man whose pale white skin was so different that many who saw him for the first time thought he was a spirit walking. "I like to think that our clan is so different that we are not of The Chosen or of The Second People. That we are the first."

"The first what?" Fox asked.

"The first of the people who are both. We are both clan and other. Gesher is of The Second People while Ibex is of The Chosen. They have a son Lynx. Fawn is Lynx's mate and they have a son."

"Yes, I do," Fawn said, standing up and sending a fast sign to Rabbit. "And so does Rabbit. We have been away from our babies since the sun rose. We have to get back so they can suckle. I know that the other mothers will share their breast milk with Badger and with Ox, but I need to hold him myself. My breasts are full and starting to ache."

"That is what I am saying," Marmot said. "Our clan, the Clan of Ibex, is the first to have both people living together in a group. We are the first."

Gesher looked at Ibex and she looked at him. "What Marmot says is true," Gesher said softly. "Our clan is not like any other. We are the first to have both The Chosen and The Second People living as one. We use words from both; we use the ways of both. What seems to be the best way, the way of The Chosen or The Second People, we have used as our way."

8

Rhino sat with the leaders of the clans and listened to the tales that Ibex, Gesher and the others from her clan were telling. He was hearing words that he never had heard before, seeing signs and signals that were familiar yet strange. But he sat there listening intently as the stories were told. Beside him sat Mammoth, and on the other side sat Deer and Boar. Behind the leaders of the clans were the men and women along with the children of the clans. The stories that were being told were so good that even the younger ones sat there quietly.

If one of the babies or the youngest of the toddlers started to fuss, the mother would mutter quietly, pick up the boy or girl and walk away after whispering to her mate or someone else to tell them what they were missing.

Ibex stood in front of the gathering and looked out at the many men and women sitting there around the campfires. "You have heard of our tales and why we are here. I could tell you even more; the new way that the males and females in our clan mate. What we do and feel when we kiss; and no, we do not bite each other on the lip. But I have talked enough. Many of us have wondered what Mammoth and the Neander Clan have to say. We heard even before they came that they were coming to tell the other clans something that was important. Mammoth would you come and tell us what it is that you traveled so far to say?"

Mammoth stood and arched his back to relieve some of the strain. He was getting old, and sitting for long periods made his backache. "Ibex tells us many things to think about," he said, as he signaled his clan to move closer. "But hear what I have to say. It is not a tale of hunting skill. It is not a story of a great adventure. It is something that I have no memory of. I have talked to the elders of the clan, and they do not remember hearing of such a thing before.

Not even the stories of when we were pulled from the ground and made men tell of such a thing. Hear what I have to say and think about what it could mean."

Boar looked at Rhino. "Do you know what he is going to say?"

Rhino shook his head from side to side and shrugged his shoulders. "Mammoth and his clan have not said what it is that they traveled so far to tell the gathering. Now we will hear."

Mammoth started to use the large sweeping gestures that meant so much to those who knew them. His arms seemed to weave and move as if they were being pushed and pulled by the spirits. His eyes were closed as if he was asleep. "The Neander Clan," he said, in a voice that was not a whisper. It was more than a whisper but not a yell. It was not the voice used to talk to someone that was close, but it was not the voice that was used to scream at someone far away. To those that knew him, it did not even sound like his voice. "The Neander Clan," he repeated, "has been in the same valleys and mountain ridges for as long as The Chosen have memories. We have lived there, hunted there, died there and the men and women who were before us have been buried there. We have done this for so many springs that we can't count."

He paused for just a few heartbeats then continued the sweeping gestures and talking in a voice that was strange and different. "Now, the Neander Clan may have to leave the homes of our ancestors. Now, we may have to travel into your valleys and mountains in order to live and raise our children."

Deer's eyebrows arched as he looked at Boar. Silently he mouthed the words as his hands sent the almost hidden message. But Lynx saw it and tapped Gesher on the shoulder. "Why would Mammoth and his people talk about leaving the valleys of their ancestors?"

"Something is happening that has never happened in our memories. Perhaps the spirits are angry, or maybe they have left us. But since I took a mate, and our two sons are now grown men, the snows come earlier and stay longer. The cold winds blow more. We are the Neander Clan we can live with cold and snow. We can't, nor could any clan, live where the animals we hunt are no more."

He paused, yet again as his arms fell toward his sides, then rose as if being pulled up by themselves. "It may be that the spirits are sending us a sign. Perhaps they are angry with our clan. But hear this, and listen to what I say. The cold and snow are forcing the animals that we hunt out of our valleys and mountains. They are leaving the ancestral hunting places that we have used since the Neander Clan first came to these mountains. You hunted mammoth here in this valley. You killed mammoth here in this valley. Has any hunter, from any clan that calls these valleys home, ever killed a mammoth before? If they have, it was not here, it was closer to where the Neander Clan lives."

Heads began to nod in agreement as the men and women huddled around the campfires listened to the words being said by Mammoth, the leader of the Neander Clan.

The whispered conversations seemed to have a life of their own as men leaned over to the one sitting next to them.

"Why have the mammoth, the Woolly Rhino, the reindeer and the other animals that we have hunted for as long as the memories exist, leave our valleys and mountains?" Mammoth slowly continued his tale as all eyes and ears again focused exclusively on him. "Have the spirits forgotten us? Are the spirits sending us a message? Do the spirits want us to do something that we are not doing? I do not know the reason, I do not have an answer. But this I do know. Many clans have women who speak to the spirits. The Neander Clan does not have a voice to talk to the spirits. But I know that some of the clans that are here at the gathering have females that talk to the spirits. I am here at the gathering to ask that the females that have the ability to talk to the spirits seek the answer to what is happening."

"I am one who talks to the spirits," Ibex said, as she looked around trying to see if there were any other women who were able to talk to the spirits. "I have the ability to talk to the spirits. Who here is also able to talk to the spirits?"

A heavyset woman pushed through the circle of people gathered around the huddled leaders. "I am called Snow Leopard. I am one who talks to the spirits." She wheezed as she walked over to Ibex. Her breathing was labored and Ibex saw the sweat pour down her face. For a few heartbeats, Ibex paused as she looked at the woman. Extending her hand in welcome, Ibex grabbed the woman's hand and squeezed. "It is good to meet you, Snow Leopard. Have you heard if there are others here who talk to the spirits?"

"Yes, there is!" a voice said, from the outer edge. "I am called Otter. I do not think that there are any more here. Three women who talk to the spirits from just five clans is a blessing. I was at a gathering five springs ago where I was the only one who spoke to the spirits, and there were three clans there."

Ibex looked around at the people that seemed to be pushing closer and closer to where they were standing. "We need someplace where we can be alone. We need to have a shelter built where we can seek the voice of the spirits."

Otter nodded her head in agreement. Turning to the large group that was standing there looking at them, she yelled. "We can't talk to the spirits in the open. The spirits only talk to us if we are able to talk to them without any one else to hear or see."

Snow Leopard looked around at the large number of people that were around them. "Go, finish butchering your kills. Make the skins into clothing. Just go!"

Ibex took Snow Leopard by the arm as if trying to use her arm to make her go somewhere. Her one hand was on the woman's wrist while her other was draped over her shoulder gently touching her upper chest. "It is good to see and talk to other women who have the ability to talk to the spirits. Are you also a medicine woman like I am?"

"No I am not." Snow Leopard replied. "You say you are a woman who talks to the sprits and who also is a medicine woman? That is almost unheard of. The skills and knowledge of a medicine woman are very special and something that is passed from mother to daughter. The ability to talk to the spirits is only given by them to a few females. It seems that you are blessed two times by the spirits."

"Perhaps I am, maybe I am not," Ibex told her, as her fingers felt for the pulse in the woman's wrist. "It seems as if the spirits are trying to use me;" at least that is what I sometimes think," Ibex said to the woman, as her experienced fingers on the other hand touched the woman's rapidly beating heart. "Does your clan have a medicine woman?" Ibex asked, as she tried to push the woman toward a stump. "Why don't we go and sit over there while the leaders try to find us a place to hold our prayer?"

"No, I am fine," The heavyset woman said, pulling away from Ibex. "I just get tired easily and sometimes it is hard to breathe."

"What is your medicine woman doing for you? Is she giving you medicines?"

"Why?" Snow Leopard asked, looking directly into Ibex's eyes.

"You have the heart problem that some people get. I felt your heart beating and the beats are not regular. There is medicine for a heart that does not beat a regular rhythm. I have more than enough in my pouches if your medicine woman needs some."

"I am fine," the big woman replied. "What we must do now is find a place where we can be alone. There must be no interruptions or distractions when we call out to the spirits. They will not come to our call if there are any other people around where we are calling to them. The spirits only come and talk to those they have chosen."

Otter saw the way the other two women who talk to the spirits were talking and touching each other. "Is there a problem?" she asked, twisting her head slightly and narrowing her gaze. "If there is a problem, then the spirits will not come and talk to us."

"Snow Leopard is ill," Ibex said quietly. "She has a problem with her heart. I can treat it if she would let me."

"She has a problem with her heart?" Otter whispered, looking first at Ibex and then at Snow Leopard. "Is it serious?"

"That is a question that I could answer better if I could look closer and feel for the hidden places where the spirits put the signs that tell when a person is sick."

"Later," Snow Leopard said, pushing Ibex and Otter away. "I do not like to say this, but I had a dream last fall, now I know it was a vision. In the dream I saw the animals leaving the places they had lived in for as long as memories have existed. The people saw them leave and wondered why. Now Mammoth comes and says that is what is happening. We must seek the answer from the spirits. They must tell us why."

Rhino walked up to the three women and tapped Snow Leopard on the shoulder. "There is a hide shelter made up for the three of you. It is beyond the bend in the river. Look for the place where the path of boulders almost crosses the river. The shelter is in a small grove of nut trees. We have started a fire for you. We have also posted guards around the shelter to keep anyone, or anything, away from you while you seek the answer. If the guards are too close, just ask them to move a few more steps. They are our most trusted hunters. Nothing, or no one will bother you while you meditate with spirits."

Ibex smiled and patted Rhino on the shoulder. "We will go and find this place where the path of boulders tries to cross the river. Is it upstream or downstream?"

"Upstream, " Rhino said. "Didn't I say that?"

"No, you didn't" Otter replied. "How far upstream?"

124

"Go to the water and it is three spear throws upstream."

"I have to get one more thing," Otter said and ran back to where she and her clan were camping.

"There it is!" Ibex said as she and the other two women who talk to the spirits saw the hide shelter. "It seems to be just right."

"I think that the men who are guarding the shelter should move about one spear throw further from the shelter," Otter said, clutching her long round bundle to her chest. "The spirits would not want anyone who is not chosen by them to hear the ceremony."

"Perhaps you are right," Snow Leopard said, glancing at the six men who were surrounding the shelter. "This will be the first time that I have ever tried to talk to the spirits when I was not in a small dark cave. I hope that they will be able to hear us in a shelter made out of hides."

"So do I," Ibex said in a whisper, which was barely heard by the other two women standing right next to her.

"They will come!" Otter said, as a smile slowly creased her face. "There is no reason to worry."

"No reason to worry?" Snow Leopard replied, looking right at the young girl. "You are young, barely a woman, how long have you been talking to the spirits?"

"I first talked to the spirits before I became a woman. They came to me in a dream that, the woman who talked to spirits in our clan said was a vision sent by the spirits. Since that heartbeat, I have been one who was chosen by them to hear what they have to tell us. Do not be fooled by my age," Otter replied calmly, "I have been visited by the spirits many times. I was taught the secret of calling them."

"Calling the spirits?" Ibex asked, looking at Otter. "I never heard of anyone being able to call the spirits."

"I heard of it, but I do not believe it!" Snow Leopard said as she gestured to the men standing guard around the hide shelter to move further away.

"You will believe it when I start to call them and they come," Otter said as she bent over and entered the shelter.

Ibex came into the shelter and sat down next to Otter. "I have the medicine plants that must be used. Do you have any?"

"Of course I do," Otter replied, glancing up as Snow Leopard crawled in. "I think I have enough for all three of us if it is needed."

"Enough of what?" Snow Leopard asked, as she sat down on the other side of Ibex.

"The secret medicine plants that those that talk to the spirits use," Ibex answered.

"Oh, those!" Snow Leopard seemed to sneer, as she replied. "Why wouldn't I have them?"

"Will you two please start a fire and prepare the medicine that we will take to help us talk to the spirits," Otter asked, as she began to unroll the oddly shaped bundle of mink furs that she had been carrying.

"I have the twirling stick and platform along with enough moss and dried grass to get the fire started," Ibex replied. "I will start the fire, Snow Leopard will you please get some firewood?"

"In a few heartbeats," the massive woman answered. "But before doing that I have to rest. My chest feels as if someone is sitting on it."

Ibex jumped to her feet and reached for her medicine bag. "Otter, go and find the medicine woman from Snow Leopard's clan. Tell her to come as fast as she can. Tell her that Snow Leopard is dying!"

"Dying?" Otter asked, glancing up at Ibex. "How can you know that? Did you talk to the spirits?"

"I know what I know," Ibex said grabbing the young woman and shoving her out of the shelter. "Remember that I am also a medicine woman of The Chosen."

Ibex spilled all of her medicines out on the ground as she looked for the few plants that could help Snow Leopard.

Gesher burst through the small opening. "Are you alright? Is something wrong? Otter ran through the gathering screaming for all the medicine women to go to the hide shelter that was made for the women who talk to the spirits. I was worried that something had happened to you!"

"I am fine, it is Snow Leopard that needs help. She is dying, or at least I think she is." Ibex said, as she continued to look through her supply of medicinal herbs and plants. "She says her chest feels as if someone is sitting on it. I am sure that it is her heart. But it is dark in here and I can't find the right medicines. Please start a fire so that I can see better."

"No, I will bring back some firewood and also a flaming branch from a fire that is already burning. That way the fire here will be started and will be burning as soon as I get back here."

"Go quickly, I fear there is only a few heartbeats left before she joins the spirits."

Gesher ducked under the flap and ran toward the gathering. Passing Wolf and the others who were coming toward him he shouted, "she is alright, Ibex is all right. It is the other woman.

Grab firewood and a burning limb from one of the fires and start one in the hide shelter. I am getting my medicine pouches."

"There," Ibex muttered under her breath, "that is what I am looking for. There seems to be more than enough Hawthorn, but should I give it to her in a drink or squeeze the juice from the plant straight into her mouth? I think I will mix it in a drink to hide the bad taste. I could also use Heal all, which is good for the heart. That has to be boiled. Where is that fire?"

At the very heartbeat that she muttered the words about the fire, Fawn crawled under the flap with a blazing limb. Behind her came Rhino with an armful of firewood. "How is she?"

"I am worried. She is just sitting there gasping and not saying anything. Where are the other medicine women?"

"I am here," a voice said, from outside the shelter. Then a thin, actually very thin, extremely short, old woman, entered the shelter. "I am called Mouse. I am the medicine woman of the Neander Clan. What is the problem?"

Ibex was about to say more when Gesher returned with his pouches, and another woman crept through behind him. "What is wrong with Snow Leopard," the new woman asked, as she stood up in the shelter. "Otter was screaming that she was dying?"

"I am not dying," Snow Leopard, said from where she was sprawled on the floor of the shelter. "I am just having problems breathing. I have been getting bigger and bigger lately, and my size is making it harder to breathe."

The new woman walked over to Snow Leopard and forced open her eyelids as far as they would go. Then she felt her chest and placed her fingers on Snow Leopard's wrist. "The spirits are unhappy," she said quietly. "They are making her heart pound as if she had been running for a long distance. "Her wrist is telling me that there is a problem. The blood passing through there is forcing its way through the veins much to fast. It should feel like a bump –

bump – bump, but it feels like bumpita, bumpita. It is very fast, way too fast for anyone except a person who had just finished running a very long distance."

"I also thought that," Ibex said, as she began to prepare the medicines that she had picked to treat Snow Leopard's rapidly beating heart. "Gesher is a healer; that is what the people he came from call those who care for the sick and injured. Gesher, will you look at her?"

Snow Leopard and the other two looked at Gesher, and the disbelief on their faces said more than words could say.

"The people where he came from have males to care for people who are injured or sick?"

Gesher bent over Snow Leopard and felt her forehead. "No, that is not right. In the places where The Second People are, both men and women care for those who are hurt or sick. It is up to the spirits to pick the healers. Few are shown the secrets of the herbs and plants that are used to make people better."

"But," Otter started to say, then stopped. "If the spirits chose you, then you are one of the chosen by them. What do you say is the matter with Snow Leopard?"

"She does not have a fever. She has not been running, but her heart is beating as if she has. The problem with Snow Leopard is that she is too fat. The fat around her waist and everywhere else on her body is making her heart beat more than is good. I would say that first we give her as much Apium as we have, or that she can eat. Does anyone still have any piss-in-bed? Or maybe a supply of horsetail? I think we need to make her pass a lot of water while we treat her heart."

"I am called Weasel, I am the medicine woman of Snow Leopard's clan. I have some horsetail and just a little piss-in-bed. But have you thought of using arbutus? I have used it to make people pass large amounts of water when it was needed."

129

"That is not a medicine I have heard of," Ibex said, glancing at the woman. "You will have to tell me more about the benefits of this plant. Where is it found and what does it look like?"

"I will tell you all about the plant. We can trade supplies of medicines and also what we know."

"Good," Ibex said, "but now the water is boiling and we need to make the medicines for her to drink."

Snow Leopard was sprawled out on the dirt of the shelter looking up at the growing group of people gathered around her. Her head was tilted upward and supported by two pairs of hands. One pair had the back of her neck where it joins the head, and the other pair of hands was lower on her neck holding more of her shoulders than neck. She was drinking and drinking and drinking the various liquids that had been made by the medicine women and by Gesher.

"I have to pass water!" She suddenly said, as she struggled to get up off the ground. "I need to get outside now!"

"Help her up," Ibex said as she grabbed a hold of Snow Leopard's arm. "Gesher help her up."

"I am able to get up and go outside myself." Snow Leopard exclaimed, as she rolled over and rose to her knees and then her feet. "I may be fat, as some think, but I am not unable to help myself when I want to do something."

"Watch her," Gesher said in a whisper that was barely heard by Ibex and Weasel. "She has had a lot of water with many kinds of medicines in the water. If she does not pass a very lot of water, then we have a different problem to treat."

"I am still worried about her heart and what we can do about it."

"We can give her medicines to make her pass water and medicines that make her not want to eat."

"That is a good plan," Ibex added, as she watched Snow Leopard pass water and then more water and then even more water.

"I think that the problem with Snow Leopard and her heart is over, at least for now." Gesher said, as he picked up his medicine pouches. "We will leave and let those who talk to the spirits try to contact them and find out what is happening."

Ibex reached up and pulled Gesher's head downward. Her lips were barely a finger length from his. "Have you noticed how everyone is starting to use the words and signs that we have been using?"

"Have you noticed," Gesher said, "how our people are beginning to use the words from the clans that are new to us?"

"Yes, I have. It is good that we are exchanging words, signs, and even new ways to do things. I have never seen the clans so eager to learn new words or signs. It is as if what we are bringing to the gathering is so new and unusual that the clans are happy to start using the new words and signs."

"I have even seen Lynx and Fawn starting to use the words that the Neander Clan is using. They are very unusual. I thought that I knew how The Chosen look, but that clan is shorter and more muscular than you or any other man or woman that I have seen from any clan that we have been with."

"You are right. The Neander Clan is different, not much that I can see, but they are different from those that live further south. But now is not good to talk about those things. Now we have to seek the spirits and try to see what it is that they are going to tell us."

"Are you coming?" The voice asked the question as Ibex and Gesher kissed each other. Then the question was changed to, "what are you doing? Are you trying to bite each other? Is that how you say goodbye?"

Ibex turned to the other women who talk with the spirits. "No, it is not what you think. In our clan we kiss each other on the lips to show that we care. Later I will explain what a kiss is and why it is important. But as you say, now it is important to try to talk to the spirits to find out why the mammoth and other animals from the north are moving south."

Otter carefully unfolded the skins that were holding her flute. She handled the bundle of skins and the flute as tenderly and as carefully as a new mother holds her firstborn for the first few heartbeats of the infant's life. Her fingers rubbed the bear's thighbone as they searched for the holes that had been drilled into the bone.

Ibex stopped what she was doing and just looked at Otter and the flute. "What is that?"

"It is the way I call the spirits to come to where I am. I was taught this by a very old woman from a clan called the Vindija. She was shown the secret of calling the spirits in a dream."

Ibex sat down next to Otter and could do nothing but stare at the bear bone with the holes drilled into it. She knew it was the bone from a bear by the way it was shaped and the size and thickness of the bone. "How does it call the spirits?"

"How it calls the spirits only the spirits know. But this I do know; when I play the music, the spirits always come. The sounds that the bear's bone makes reminds me of the sounds a bird would try to make. It is like a bird's call to a mate, yet different. I place my fingers on the holes like this. Then by blowing into this end, and moving my fingers so that some cover the holes while some are lifted off the holes, I can make different sounds. It is very hard to make, and takes many days to learn how to make the sounds that call the spirits."

Ibex sat there and could barely talk or even think. A way to call the spirits to come would be very good, and it would be even better when combined with the drink that only those who talk with the spirits know how to make. Shaking her head slowly from side to side she tried to think of what to do. "I will make the drink that we need to drink to help us talk to the spirits," she said softly. "Otter would you please start to make the sounds on that bear bone to call the spirits."

9

The three women who talked to the spirits sat and slowly sipped the foul tasting liquid that was made from the secret plants that only they knew. They had used leaves from some plants, stems from other plants, roots and even fungi mixed together in a secret way that was only known to those who were trained to talk to the spirits. It was a secret that was sacred to them and they would prefer to die before sharing it with anyone who was not one of them.

Ibex could not take her eyes off the bear thighbone that Otter was using to make strange, yet very pleasing to the ear, sounds. She sipped her drink and sat and listened to the sounds that were coming from the bone under Otter's moving fingers.

Otter sat in the center of the shelter and closed her eyes. Her fingers seemed to move as if they were being pulled and pushed by the very spirits that she was calling. Her body gently swayed back and forth to the mellow tones that emanated from the bone.

Ibex took another sip, and then another, of the drink that helped them talk to the spirits. Why she did what she did next, only they knew, but she closed her eyes and began to sway back and forth. The sounds of the bone flute seemed to fill her mind.

Snow Leopard closed her eyes as the secret potion began to make her sleepy. The sounds, coming from the bear bone with the holes drilled in it, helped to make her unaware of the surroundings in which the three women were sitting. As if being pulled and pushed by unseen forces, her body began to sway back and forth.

Outside the shelter, where the men who were standing guard were, Wolf looked at Lynx and motioned to him. "What is that sound? It is not any animal or bird that I know? Do you recognize the sound?"

Lynx shook his head back and forth and shrugged his shoulders. "It is strange, it is something that I have not heard before. I have been listening to it and trying to identify what it is."

Rhino and Mammoth stood a spear throw away from where Lynx and Wolf were standing guard. "The sound seems to be coming from the shelter where the three women who talk to the spirits are. What do you think the sounds are?" Rhino asked.

"It is not any animal that I know, it is not any bird I have ever heard. Perhaps it is the sounds of the spirits coming to the shelter to talk to the women."

Wolf heard what was said and began to move further away from the shelter. "If it is the sounds of the spirits, I think that we should move further away. I have never heard the spirits, but I think that they would not want us so close to the shelter when they talk to the spirit women."

Lynx also started to move away from the shelter. "I think you are right, the spirits would not want us so close. If we can hear those sounds we are too close. We have to get further away."

All around the shelter made of stretched skins over a framework of limbs and branches, the men who were guarding the shelter moved further and further away. "We can't go any more," Mammoth said as he signaled the rest of the men. "Even if the sounds can still be heard, we have to stay where we are. If we go further, we will not be able to see one another and will not be able to guard the shelter. Someone could sneak in and interrupt the ceremony."

Inside the shelter, Ibex, Snow Leopard and Otter continued to sip the drink while Otter played the bear bone flute. The smoke from the fire wafted up toward the top of the shelter and began to fill the small enclosure.

Otter's fingers moved slowly over the holes that had been so carefully drilled into the thighbone of the cave bear. She gently blew into the open end of the bone while her fingers continued to cover then uncover the various holes. As her fingers closed some of the holes and other holes were left uncovered by her fingers the sounds changed. Some were high pitched while others were low. But regardless of which, high or low, the sounds were pleasing to the ears of the women gathered there and soothing.

"They are here," Snow Leopard suddenly whispered, "I can feel them. The sounds have brought the spirits."

Ibex felt a shiver race down her spine as she also felt that the spirits had come. "Yes," she said softly "they are here."

Otter stopped playing the flute and lifted her drink to her lips. Three massive gulps of the liquid and it was finished. "Drink it all now," she told the other two. "You have to finish the special drink now so that the spirits can talk to us."

Ibex nodded and slurped the remaining fluid as rapidly as she could. She noticed that Snow Leopard was quietly gagging on her drink but was swallowing as fast as she could. The special drink was made to be sipped slowly, not swallowed rapidly. But if the spirits had already come, the remaining potion had to be finished.

The three women who talked to the spirits sat there with the smoke from the fire slowly filling the shelter that had been made for them. Otter again picked up the flute and began to finger the holes nervously. Inhaling as deeply as she could she blew into the end of the flute. She placed all of her fingers over the holes then lifted one finger. As she replaced that finger she lifted another finger. Then she lifted two at the same time, and then she covered them as she lifted the other two fingers. Pausing for a few heartbeats she whispered to the spirits, "We are three women who talk to the spirits, we welcome you here and wait for you to talk to us." She waited another few heartbeats then again began playing the flute.

136

Ibex waited for a few more heartbeats before she could say anything. She wanted to talk, to ask the spirits what was happening, but suddenly her mouth felt as if she had not had anything to drink for many days. Her tongue seemed to be stuck to the top of her mouth. Her lips were dry and she kept licking them trying to get them moist. But she had to ask, "What is happening?" Her voice sounded as if it was the voice of a stranger. She did not even think that she had said the words. The voice that had asked the questions could not have been hers. It seemed to be an echo from far away. "Why have the mammoth and the reindeer and other animals from the north started to move south?" The ringing in her ears grew in intensity and the echo was even further away. "Are the clans from the north in danger?"

Snow Leopard opened her mouth to ask a question but no words came out. She tried to think of what to say but couldn't think of how to ask her questions. The ringing in her ears grew louder and louder. Even with her eyes clenched closed she could still see.

Otter stopped playing her bear bone flute and looked up at the top of the shelter. She saw how the smoke from the fire was slowly circling above her head. Then her ears started to ring and even with her eyes shut she saw something.

Ibex waited patiently for an answer to her questions. Why didn't the spirits talk to her? She tried to stand so that she could walk closer to where Snow Leopard was sitting. No wait, Snow Leopard was no longer sitting, she was flat on her back and was not moving. Is she dead Ibex thought? Did her heart stop beating? No, she realized, she was breathing. Her chest was expanding and contracting with each breath that she took.

Ibex tried to talk to Otter but as her head turned toward the woman, she saw that Otter was quietly lying on her back with her eyes tightly shut. She started to say something but couldn't think of what to say to either the spirits or to the other two women that were lying there as if they were sleeping. The smoke was making her eyes water, she felt the tears running down her cheeks and dripping off her chin. She was starting to feel dizzy and her stomach was churning as if she was about to vomit. I have to lie down she thought, I have to get on my back so that the smoke does not make my eyes water and so that I will not be dizzy. That is what I tell a woman who is expecting to do when they tell me that they are dizzy in the morning and feel like vomiting. Is that why Otter and Snow Leopard are on their backs? They would know what she knows and that should be why they are flat on their backs. Ibex smiled and laid down on the hard ground of the shelter.

Even with her eyes clenched tightly, shut to keep the stinging smoke from making her eyes water, Ibex saw the thin wispy forms above her. They moved back and forth, they moved up and down, they were above her then they were not. They opened their mouths, was that really a mouth? She heard the muffled sobbing but couldn't move her head to see who, or what, was sobbing. She heard moaning but did not know who was moaning.

Otter lay on her back listening to the sounds around her. Someone was sobbing and someone was moaning. She tried to see who it was but couldn't. It was as if someone, or something, had her head clamped firmly in place so that she couldn't move her head. All she could see through her closed eyelids were the small darting forms that moved through the smoke. Her eyes were closed as tightly as she could clamp them together, but still she could see the moving forms that floated above her.

Snow Leopard clutched her belly and fought the urge to vomit. Her stomach was churning and she could feel the burning bile pushing up into her throat. She struggled to open her eyes but couldn't. However, even with her eyes shut against the smoke that was filling the shelter, she saw the outlines of the spirits above her. They swarmed though the smoke like the moths around the smoke from the campfires of The Chosen. They opened their mouths and began to talk to her. She heard them and the message that they brought made her gasp in fear.

Otter twisted slightly as the forms above her seemed to fly straight toward her. She heard them speaking even though they did not open their mouths. What they were saying sent a shiver of dread racing down her spine.

Ibex tried to cover her eyes to help keep the smoke out of her eyes. But even with her fingers covering her eyes she could see the transparent shapes of the spirits above her. They loomed above her and seemed to be pointing their fingers right at her. She heard what they were saying and the words they spoke were frightening.

Gesher stood at the far edge of the clearing where the shelter was and saw the smoke begin to seep out of the shelter. It oozed like wet mud from between the edges of the hides that were used as a covering for the shelter. It poured out of the sides of the hide that was used as an entrance. As he watched the smoke curling skyward he began to worry about Ibex and the other two women. He knew that smoke could kill. It was one of the silent killers that no one knew was coming. It could be the smoke from a massive fire that was burning vast forests or it could be from a smoldering fire in a shelter where no one was watching what was burning.

Motioning for Rhino to come closer he began to whisper in the man's ear. "What do you think about all the smoke coming out of the shelter? I have never been around a ceremony where anyone was talking to the spirits. Have you?"

"I have been at ceremonies like this," Rhino said quietly as he also glanced over at the smoke seeping out of the shelter. "I do know that the women who talk to the spirits isolate themselves in a shelter like the one we made. They make a fire and do other things that only they know how, or what, to do. That is why they are the ones who talk to the spirits."

"So the smoke coming out from between the hides that are covering the shelter is what should be?"

"It does seem to be a little more than I have seen before, but the shelter has three women in it, not just one."

Gesher was about to turn around and again scan the forest edge when a large spark burned its way through the hide covering, sputtered for a heartbeat and then died. The air was filled with the acrid smell of burning hide as yet another spark burned through in another place.

"Fire!" He screamed. "Fire in the shelter."

Even before the last words were spoken he was running toward the shelter. "Ibex," he yelled as he neared the shelter. "Ibex, the shelter is burning, you have to get out."

Behind him the rest of the men who were guarding the shelter against any possible interruption of the ceremony rushed toward the shelter. The yells of the men brought the rest of the people from the clans running toward the shelter.

"We have to get them out! someone yelled.

"I can see more places where the hides are starting to smolder," another voice screamed.

"There is so much smoke inside that I can't see them!" Wolf screamed, as he pushed aside the flap covering the opening.

Lynx pushed past him and dropped to his knees. "I can feel someone," he shouted. "I have her, whoever she is, grab my legs and pull us out."

Rhino grunted as he pulled on Lynx's legs. "Help me," he shouted.

Fawn crawled into the smoke filled interior of the shelter and felt along the ground until she brushed against an inert form. "I found someone," she started to yell but the smoke filled her lungs and she started to cough. Grasping the outstretched arm she tried to pull whoever it was out of the smoke. As she struggled with the weight of the person she started to feel woozy and lightheaded. Her coughing intensified and she had problems breathing.

140

She felt someone brush against her leg and reached out. Her fingers brushed the hair of someone. "I am here," she coughed grabbing the person's arm. "I found someone." She coughed as the heavy smoke filled her lungs and made her eyes water. "Here, follow my arm and you will feel her." She was coughing so badly that nearly every word was broken by a series of coughs. But she felt the hands move down her am and the contact of the hand with hers on the person's arm.

The shelter suddenly burst into flames and the heat from the flames intensified driving the rescuers out of the ceremonial shelter. Coughing and shaking their heads the men and women tried to clear their eyes and lungs of the deadly smoke.

Mammoth rubbed his eyes and tried to see if all of his clan members were there. But his eyes were still watering so badly that he couldn't see the faces of those standing around the burning ceremonial hut. He was about to start calling out names when a voice filled the air.

"We have to give thanks to the spirits, all three of the women who talk to the spirits are alive."

Otter coughed and started to vomit as her lungs fought to rid themselves of the deadly effects of the smoke. She felt the hands around her waist holding her stomach as she emptied her belly on the ground. Her legs buckled under her, and if the hands had not been there holding her up, she would have collapsed onto the ground. Shaking her head she fought to clear her mind.

Ibex was sprawled on the ground gasping for breath. Each breath was a struggle as her lungs fought to clear themselves of the smoke. She would inhale and immediately begin to cough so violently that she never had the ability to finish completely filling her lungs.

Snow Leopard lay on the ground with a group of people gathered around her. Her breathing was so shallow that those closest to her could barely see her chest moving as she tried to breathe.

"We have to move them further away from the fire," Fawn shouted, as she put her arm around Ibex and started to pull her away from the fire. "There is still too much smoke here."

"The fire has to be put out before it spreads to the grass and brush," Boar shouted, to be heard, as he began to beat on the flames. "Grab whatever you have to put the fire out. If you have any water in a carrier pour it on the edges of the fire to keep it from spreading."

Deer signaled his people and they all began to beat at the flames. A few of the people had water carriers, long pieces of gut that had been carefully washed and cleaned before being used to hold water. Other people were running back to the campfires for more water carriers.

Mouse bent over the inert form of Snow Leopard and shook her head. She leaned lower and placed her fingers on the woman's neck and felt for the pulsing throb of the blood as it pushed through her neck. Her other hand rested on Snow Leopard's chest feeling the throbbing beat of her heart. The rhythm was unusual and Mouse recognized the signs. "The signs are not good," she muttered under her breath. "If she lives until the sunrise the spirits will be kind."

Otter turned to Ibex and pointed toward Snow Leopard. "She is too sick to talk to us right now. But I think that we need to go somewhere and talk about what the spirits said. I saw them in the smoke. They were talking to me and telling me many secrets."

Ibex nodded quietly and motioned to Otter to follow her. "I have never seen so many spirits in the haze of the smoke. Your bear bone flute is, or was, the best way to bring the spirits to the ceremony. Is your flute safe?"

"Of course it is. The flute is always at my side and carried in a protective bundle of hides. The bundle is tied to my waist. When they pulled me out of the fire, the bundle with the flute was pulled out with me."

"I have to learn how to make one of them," Ibex whispered as she moved deeper into the forest. "It helped bring the spirits, and many spirits, to the ceremony."

"I will help you make one, but it should be the large thigh bone of an adult cave bear," Otter said as she walked into the forest.

"This is a good place to sit and talk," Ibex said, as she brushed twigs, leaves, small branches and stones out of the way.

"So, what did the spirits tell you," Otter asked, as she finished clearing a place to sit.

"It was not a good message that they brought me. I just hope that the leaders of the clans will listen," Ibex sighed, as she leaned back against a tall pine tree. "In the dreams that they sent me, the messages that they sent in the dreams could be very hard for some of The Chosen to believe."

"My dreams were also very disturbing. The messages that the spirits sent to me in my dreams told of terrible storms. I had one dream where the snowstorms never stopped. It was just one snow storm followed by another snowstorm and then more." Otter looked at the older woman sitting beside her.

"My dreams told of cold and ice along with snow," Ibex said looking at Otter and seeing the look in the young woman's eyes. "They also told of the winters getting colder and the snow staying on the ground longer."

Otter nodded her head in agreement and sighed. "I had one vision, or dream, where the valleys, where The Chosen have lived for as long as there are memories, had no animals in them. The caves of The Chosen were empty. The shelters made of animal bones and covered with the hides of those animals who died to feed The Chosen were not to be seen."

143

Ibex shook her head silently as she again remembered the images that she had seen in her dreams. She did not like to think of what the messages from the spirits were trying to tell them. "We have to go to the leaders of the clans and tell them of what we dreamt."

"I think we should talk to Snow Leopard first," Otter said. "I would like to hear what she saw in her dreams. If she did not have the same dreams, if the spirits sent her other visions of what will be, then our dreams, or visions could be wrong."

"No," Ibex said, glancing directly at Otter. I think we need to call for a gathering of the elders, the leaders, and the medicine women. And it has to be done quickly. If Snow Leopard saw the visions we saw, good. If she did not," Ibex paused and drew in a deep breath. "If she did not," she repeated, "both you and I did. That is at least two of the women who talk to the spirits who had the same visions and dreams. We must tell the others of what we saw."

10

Otter sat on one side of the fire and Ibex sat on the other side. Between them sat the leaders of the clans, the revered elders, both male and female, and the medicine women.

Rhino shook his head from side to side. "It cannot be," he kept saying. "The homes of The Chosen have been the same for as long as our memories. Why would the spirits send such a message?"

Deer nodded his head up and down in agreement. "I think that it is a message that the women who talk to the spirits misunderstood. The spirits would not do that to The Chosen. We have been their people for as long as we have lived."

Mammoth sat there watching the other leaders argue about what the dreams, or perhaps they could be called visions, meant. Slowly he began to get more and more upset over the argument between men that he had known for nearly as long as he had been alive. But he sat there listening without saying anything. He knew what he wanted to say, but was waiting for the others to finish what they wanted to say.

Boar stood and slammed the butt of his spear into the ground, or actually firmly onto the surface of a large rock, to get the attention of those at the gathering. "I worry that the spirits will leave our side and not watch over The Chosen if we do not hear the message that they sent. But we have to hear it as it was intended to be. A message sent in a dream that is mistaken is a dream that has no message for The Chosen."

Gesher waited patiently for the other leaders to speak. Even though he was the leader, or co-leader of The Clan of Ibex, he was not born one of The Chosen. He was a member of The Chosen by choice. He had the right to speak but did not want to be one of the first to talk about what Ibex and Otter had seen in their dreams.

Mouse stood and waited for the others to stop talking. Finally the mutterings and murmurings ceased as the other people became aware of her standing there. "I am a medicine woman, and I have been taking care of Snow Leopard ever since she and Ibex and Otter breathed in so much smoke. She is still very sick and can't join us at the fires while we talk about the dreams that the spirits sent us. But she has whispered to me, in between her severe coughing, about the dreams that the spirits sent her. She is upset over the messages that came in the dreams. She wants the leaders and the elders to know that she saw snowstorms in her dreams, and not just storms, but snowstorms so bad that the light and warmth that the sun brings is no more."

"It can't be, it could not happen." Rhino seemed to explode in anger, as his face began to turn the color of the sun when it was at the highest it could be on a clear summer day. "The sun has always been here keeping us warm. Even in the worst days of winter, when the winds blow the snow into large drifts, we can be secure in our knowledge that soon the sun will again bring us light to see and warmth for our faces."

Boar looked at Mouse and glared. "I do not believe the dreams that Ibex and Otter have told us about. I do not think that they understood the messages in the dreams."

Mammoth finally stood and yelled for attention. "I have been sitting here listening to these words from all of you and I do not understand what, or why, the words that Ibex and Otter spoke are not believed. You have hunted mammoth here in these woods. Have you ever hunted mammoth here in these woods? I tell you this and you should hear what I say. Something is making the large animals, the mammoth, the reindeer, the Woolly Rhino, the ox and others leave our ancestral home and travel south."

"It is because you hunted them to hard," Deer shouted. "You have to let them forget about being hunted for a moon or two before

146

hunting them again. Kill only what you need for food, clothing and shelter. Never kill more than you need and the animals will not leave your valleys."

Mammoth shouted back as loudly as he could, "do not tell me about hunting and what to do or not to do. I have been leading hunting parties ever since I was made the leader of the Neander Clan. I know what to do and what not to do. After a kill is made we do not go into that area for at least a moon perhaps even longer."

Deer's face started to turn the color of the sun. "Perhaps you have the forgetting disease of the old ones. Perhaps you think you do not hunt there for a moon but you do. That scares the animals and they seek new foraging places."

Gesher looked at Ibex and shook his head. Sending her a brief series of hand signals as he mouthed the words he rose to his feet. "I don't like what I am hearing. This is not good."

Ibex nodded her head in agreement then turned to those still sitting and also the men standing there arguing over how to hunt. "We have heard what Mammoth had to say, and also the words of the other leaders of the clans that are here at the gathering. I want to thank the leaders for including the Clan of Ibex in the gathering. Now we are leaving."

"Leaving, why leave now?" Boar asked, jumping to his feet. "It has been good having you and your clan here. The trade has been better than expected. You, and your people, have taught us many new things. New spear points so we can spear the massive sturgeon and many new words to help explain many things."

"And you, along with all the other people here, have shown us new ways to make shelters using hides stretched over bones and limbs. We have learned new words, especially from the Neander Clan. It is the Neander Clan that has been the ones to show us the most new ways of doing things and given us the most new words. Now we have words for all four seasons. But, I think that Mammoth is right, even though I can hear that the others do not. Something is

147

wrong. The spirits have sent a message to Snow Leopard, Otter and me in our dreams. We have told you what the dreams were and how we interpreted what the spirits told us in the dreams."

"But that is not a reason to leave," Boar said, as he grasped her hand.

"The Clan of Ibex is a wandering clan. We do not have a valley to call our home. We do not have mountain ridges to call our home." Gesher said, as he moved closer to Ibex. "We travel as the spirits direct. We go east, we go south, we go west and we go north. We follow rivers, we follow mountain ridges, and we travel as the spirits send us. It is a dangerous life, it is a life filled with adventure and uncertainty, but it is the way of our clan."

Ibex took Gesher's hand and gave it a squeeze. "It is the life we have chosen. Mammoth, if you and your people are being forced out of your home region because the animals are leaving, you are welcome to join us. It is a hard life, not having a place to call home, but we prefer it to staying in one valley. We have found many new people by traveling. That is how we learn new words, new ways of doing things, and can show them how we do things and teach them our words."

Mammoth shook his head from side-to-side. "I will tell my people of what you have said. But I do not think anyone will leave the Neander Clan to join yours. We are a proud people, and have stayed where we are for many moons, so many moons that we can't count, or know, how long."

Moon walked over to where Ibex was standing. The young woman, barely old enough to be called a woman, touched Ibex on the shoulder. "Woolly Rhino is sick. He would not come to you and ask for anything. He thinks he will get better soon. But I am worried."

Ibex glanced at Moon then back toward where Woolly Rhino and the men were sitting. "What is wrong with your mate?"

"At night, when we are sleeping, I hear him moan. Not much, but a few times during the night. At first I thought it was just a man thing, you know how they are always making strange noises. But I have noticed that he is now even doing it when he is awake."

Ibex nodded and whispered to the young woman. "That may be right, but have you noticed that we, the females, also make noises sometimes? What exactly is the moan and when does he do it?"

"I don't know, a moan is a moan."

"No there are many different moans. Gesher moans in pleasure when we make love."

"I have seen that. Tell me why you call it making love, we have always called it mating."

"It took me many seasons of new growth, or springs as some call it, to realize what Gesher was saying when he was talking about loving me. He kept saying that he loved me when he was kissing me or when we were mating. We had been together as mates for many moons when I started to understand what he was talking about, what the word love really meant."

"So what is this love? What does it mean?"

Ibex paused as she tried to think of what to say. Love as a feeling was hard to explain. At least it was hard to explain until you realized the feeling yourself.

Drawing in a deep breath she motioned Moon to sit. "Love is a feeling. The only way I could try to tell you is that when you do

149

realize that you love your mate, then that feeling will be like nothing you have ever known. When that happens, then you will begin to call mating making love. That will be when you start saying you are making love and not just mating. When you really love your mate you will want to make him happy and want to do what makes him happy. When he loves you, he will want to do the same. Rabbit just started calling it making love. It has taken her many moons to realize what love is."

"So," Moon said, as her head turned toward where Rabbit was sitting, "Rabbit called it mating for many moons?"

"As did all the others, except for Lynx and Fawn. They grew up knowing what love was and what it means. The others had to be shown and taught. They watched, they listened, they learned. You will too."

"I don't know. Woolly Rhino is my mate, but he is not like Gesher or Lynx or even Fox. I see how they are with their mates. He is not like them. He does not even like to kiss me. That is one of the things that you showed the clans at the gathering. Kissing is fun; I want to be kissed all the time. Now that I think about it, we thought that you and the others in your clan were chewing or at least biting the lips of the other person."

Ibex started to laugh then stopped herself by gently biting her lower lip. "Kissing should be fun. The more Gesher kisses me the more I want to make love." She paused for a heartbeat before saying anything more. "Perhaps the problem is you. Do you kiss him or just let him kiss you?"

"He kisses me but he does not seem to like doing it."

"Then it is up to you to make it more enjoyable for him. Make your lips soft, don't push hard against his lips. Move your tongue around just inside his mouth. Open your mouth just wide enough for him to get his tongue inside your mouth. Flick your tongue against his. Use your tongue to caress the roof of his mouth and the edges of his lips. You are both young, you were not even mates when you left the Neander Clan to join our clan."

"We were not mates," Moon replied nodding her head up and down. "But as soon as we decided to leave the Neander Clan and join your clan, we spoke to each other and Gesher named us a mated pair."

"That was three moons ago, nearly four moons I think, since we left the gathering and again started our trek. Neither you or Woolly Rhino had shared a sleeping place with anyone before joining our clan. He is still a young man in many ways, and you are a young woman. Listen to my words and think of what will be." Ibex placed her hands on the young woman's shoulder. "But enough of this female talk. Let me go and see what is wrong with your mate."

Woolly Rhino looked up and then stood up as Ibex came toward him. The look that he directed toward Moon carried a message that was not lost on Ibex.

"As the medicine woman of the clan I am asking that you let me examine you."

"I am not sick, I have no wounds, why would you want to examine me?"

Your mate has said that you are moaning in your sleep. A moan can mean many things. If there is something wrong, then as the leader of the clan and also the medicine woman, I must know."

"I told you," he replied scowling at Ibex and at Moon, "I am not sick!" His voice started to take on just a slight hint of anger.

"Gesher," Ibex said as she motioned to her mate, "would you come here?"

Gesher walked over and Lynx followed. "What do you want?"

151

"As a leader of the clan, and the elder male plus a healer, would you look at Woolly Rhino? He does not want me to examine him, but Moon says she is worried about him. That he moans in his sleep and even when waking. I was going to look at him to try to see what could be wrong, but he will not let me."

"Not let you!" Lynx exclaimed looking right at Woolly Rhino. "No one in this clan has ever said that you could not examine them. You are the medicine woman of the clan."

Gesher towered over Woolly Rhino as he did all the males from The Chosen. But as he placed his hands on his hips, he rose to the very tips of his toes to make himself even taller. "Is there any reason that you would not want your leader, and your medicine woman, to try to find out if you are sick? Is there?"

"No," Woolly Rhino stammered, glancing at the rest of the clan moving closer to where he was standing. "But I do not think I am sick. I do moan a lot. It has even made me wake up when I did it. But it is not serious, or even because I am sick. It just happens."

"But your mate is worried about you, and she cares enough about you to worry and to let me know that she is worried. That is reason enough for me to want to look at you to see if there is something wrong. But I will not, if you do not want me too."

"Please," Moon said, grabbing him by the arm, "let her look at you. If you are not sick, or do not have a wound, why are you moaning? I just want to be sure that you are not sick."

Woolly Rhino looked at his mate, he glanced at the rest of the clan gathered around where he was standing and he saw the look in their eyes. Did he dare not have Ibex look at him? Drawing in a deep breath he nodded his head up and down. "If that is what Moon wants, then I will do what she wants."

Ibex looked at Gesher and smiled. "Perhaps both of us should examine him. If we both look him over very carefully and find nothing wrong then he was right and Moon is wrong."

"Yes, that is a good plan. We will both look to see if there is anything wrong. I think we should start with his belly and chest." Gesher said, as he motioned to Woolly Rhino to come with him.

Gesher and Ibex poked and prodded Woolly Rhino. They pried open his eyes as far as they could stretch the lids. They opened his mouth and looked at his tongue and the top of his mouth. They stuck a very thin piece of stone into his mouth and poked at the roots of his teeth. They pushed on his belly and up under his ribs. They felt along the sides of his neck and under his arms.

Ibex asked him to roll over and she lifted his feet. She pushed on the bottom of his feet and twisted his toes. She squeezed the muscles of his legs and the kneecaps.

Gesher felt along his spine and the back of his hips. His fingers even worked their way through his thick hair feeling for anything that could be hidden in the black hair of the man's back and head.

Glancing at Ibex, Gesher silently shook his head from side to side then shrugged his shoulders.

Ibex was about to say that she had not found anything when her fingers brushed against Woolly Rhino's elbow and he moaned. It was a slight moan, barely noticeable. But both Gesher and Ibex heard it and looked at each other.

Ibex grabbed his arm with one hand and began to feel along the elbow with the other one. Gesher had Woolly Rhino's other arm clasped in a hand and was beginning to run his free hand along the man's arm. It was the elbow that Ibex was holding that made the man grimace in pain as she moved her fingers along the joint.

"It is the elbow of his left arm," Ibex said as she continued to manipulate the joint. "I can feel that it is swollen, but only a little."

"I can't notice any swelling in any other joints," Gesher said, as his fingers moved along the joints of the shoulders and down the arm

153

to the wrist. We already checked his legs. There was no swelling in the leg joints."

"He is young, barely a man, why would he be starting to have the joint aches?"

"I don't know," Gesher said as he reached over to feel the joint of the left arm. "It is usually in the knees of old men and women."

"Woolly Rhino," Ibex said, looking at the young man as she dropped his arm, letting it fall to his side. "You are starting to get the disease of the joints. You are young; I have never seen anyone as young as you with swollen joints. It is just starting, and it will be many birthing seasons, or springs, before you ache too much to be able to travel very far. I can give you some medicine that will help. But you have to let me, or Gesher, know if the ache starts to bother you in any other joints."

"Willow would be good," Gesher said as he started to think of what to give Woolly Rhino. "Or perhaps Bitterwort, or even Anthemis Nobilis."

"They are good," Ibex said in agreement, "but there is also Fenigreek and Verbena."

"Verbena, yes that is good. I think we should start with Verbena and Willow."

"I agree," Ibex said nodding. "Now lets go and tell Moon that there was something wrong with her mate and that it is good that she told me."

Gesher looked at Woolly Rhino and smiled. "Now that we have found something wrong, even if it is not serious, I think you should go back to your sleeping place and take Moon in your arms and tell her that she was right."

The early morning light was just breaking on the eastern horizon when the clan again started its journey. Gesher and Ibex were in the front of the clan setting a strong pace. Woolly Rhino and Moon were in the back of the line.

"I can't believe that I was told that they wanted me to watch the back trail."

"Why not?" Moon asked, as she quickened her pace to keep up with those moving in front of her.

"We have not been members of this clan for even four moons. To be picked as the one who must watch the back trail for danger is not something that the leader gives to a new member of a clan. Even if I was the son of the leader, a male of the leader's heart, to be asked to watch the back trail is usually given to an experienced older hunter."

"I know," Moon said, glancing back at her mate and remembering last night, and the way that he had mated with her. Maybe that was what Ibex called making love. It was different than they had ever mated before. He had seemed to change, become more eager to mate when she had pushed his lips open with her tongue and licked the inside of his lips then the upper part of his mouth. And they had been face to face. That had been a big change from what they had done before. She liked mating in the face-to-face position and kissing while mating. No, she thought, it was making love because she was now positive that she did love him.

"Yes," she nearly shouted as she twisted around to look at him. The feeling that Ibex had tried to tell her of she now understood. She loved her mate.

She paused for a heartbeat to let him catch up to where she was. But he was not moving. He had crouched down and was looking back toward the north and his spear had been raised and was pointing that way. His whistle of alarm froze all the people in their tracks.

Fox edged back to where Woolly Rhino was kneeling. "What is it? What did you see or hear?"

155

"It looked like the wisp of smoke from a campfire, but now I do not see it."

"Keep looking," Fox whispered. "I will go and tell Gesher and Ibex. They will be back here in just a few heartbeats."

"There," Fawn exclaimed, as she pointed toward a small wisp of smoke breaking the tops of the trees. But as quickly as she pointed, the smoke dissipated in the breeze.

But it was enough for Ibex to see the direction in which Fawn had pointed. "It was smoke from a campfire, or even a small encampment. We should be there in one day, or even before the sun sets, if we do not have to go too far out of the way because of swamps or thick woods that we can not get through."

11

Chamois squatted over the small indentation in the dirt. He dropped to one knee and then both knees. Then he crouched even lower as he studied the print.

"What is it?" Mountain Goat asked, as she watched what her mate was doing. "Why is that one hoof mark making you look so carefully at it?"

Star glanced up at her mother then over toward her Dada. Tugging at her mother's fur covering the young girl pointed toward her father. "Dada is looking at the track."

"Yes, he is," the woman answered. "There is something about it that is not right."

"Why?" the little girl asked, as she moved closer to where the man was studying the track.

"You will know when you start to learn the skills of the hunter and tracker, we will teach you."

"Why?"

"It is what you must learn so that you can help provide food for your hearth and your band."

"Why?"

"That is what men and women do."

"Why?"

Chamois glanced up from where he was now flat on his belly looking at the track. "Enough of asking why! Just listen to what your mother says and learn. You can learn more by watching what is done than asking why?"

She was about to ask why when she saw the scowl that her father sent toward her before he again looked at the track. Her open mouth that was ready to ask why yet again shut and she turned her back on him.

"I don't like the looks of this track. It is different from any animal that I have ever tracked. I thought that I caught sight of a strange track back about three spear throws ago. Now I see this one, but it is not a complete track."

Mountain Goat motioned for Star to stay close to her, then walked over to where her mate was gazing at the imprint in the dirt. Taking a quick glance back to make sure that Star was close by and safe, she knelt next to the track. Bending over, she cleared her nose and then inhaled deeply. Then she opened her mouth and tasted the scent with her tongue. "I don't recognize the scent."

"I don't either, it is a strange new scent that is unknown to me."

"It is only a partial track, not a full track, but it is huge. I think it is a deer."

"It looks like a deer track, what there is of it. But if it is a deer track, then it has to be a giant." Chamois looked up at his mate and smiled. "And if it is a deer, it will feed us and provide enough skin for much clothing."

"Do you realize what you have been saying?" she asked, as he got to his feet.

"What?"

"You have been talking using the new words that we learned when that band came and stayed with us when we were all sick.

158

Remember how they stayed with us, and the medicine woman who was called Ibex said that the water was bad and that is why we were all sick?"

"I remember, and they sent out a hunting party to bring back fresh meat for us to eat and fresh skins to make clothes. They killed a large deer; I think I heard them call it a megaloceros. Do you think that this is the track of a megaloceros?"

"What else could it be?"

Chamois and Mountain Goat continued to follow the twisting game trail that meandered through the broad flat valley that ran between the mountain peaks. The tall grasses intermixed with short brush and waving grains made a mosaic of various colors and designs. As the sun began to set in the west, Chamois held up his hand in the hunter's sign that said stop. "It is getting dark and we need to find a place to stay that will be safe."

"Where could that be?" Mountain Goat asked, as she looked around. "There are no caves in which we could stay. There isn't even a tall tree close by that we could climb."

"We will have to build an enclosure out of thorn bushes."

"I don't think that there are enough thorn bushes here to make a shelter," Mountain Goat said, as she broke off a long branch that was full of thorns.

"It will have to do," Chamois said, as he sliced off a large branch with his hand knife.

"Do you think that we should go back?"

"Go back?" The look that he sent his mate was reflected in the bewilderment in his eyes. "How could we go back?"

"We still could still go back, I think."

"No, we couldn't. After we said that we were leaving to follow the trail that Wolf and Rabbit traveled with Gesher and Ibex and their band, we were laughed at."

"They called it a clan," Mountain Goat said quietly.

"What? Oh yes, you're right. They did not call themselves a band of The Second People. They called themselves a clan of The Chosen."

"We should have left when Rabbit and Wolf left."

"You were too sick to travel."

"If you had asked, they may have waited for us. Rabbit was the one woman in the whole band that I could just talk to. She would sit and listen to anything I wanted to say for as long as I talked."

"Quiet, listen, what was that?" Chamois said, as he grabbed a spear.

"Something broke something and it snapped," Mountain Goat said, as she picked up Star with one arm and began to balance a spear in the other. Her fingers moved slowly on the shaft bouncing it ever so slightly as she felt for the best balancing spot.

The snapping off to their right made both of them turn their heads to try to see what was moving in the tall grasses that surrounded them.

"Hold Star tight and then press your back up against mine," Chamois said, as he grasped one spear in his right hand in the throwing position while holding another firmly in his left in the stabbing position. "Don't try to throw your spear while holding her, if she wiggles even a little as you throw, it will make the spear miss the target. Keep it ready and in the stabbing position. Do you have a club?"

"No, I don't have a club. Do you?"

"I have a club and two spears. Here take my club."

"Then you will not have a club."

"Take it!" Chamois seemed to growl, as he spoke to her. "You need two weapons to defend yourself and Star. If the spear shaft breaks when you stab, then all you will have is the club. I have a spear to throw and a spear to thrust with. I also can use both hands. You have to hold Star with one arm while defending yourself and her. Take the club!"

Mountain Goat paused for a few heartbeats as she tried to reach the club that her mate was trying to get to her. "I have to put Star down to take the club. But I am afraid that she will start to walk off as soon as she feels the ground under her feet."

"No, you don't," he said quietly, as he strained to hear any sounds on the gently blowing air. "Balance the spear against your thigh and take the club. Then put it in the belt around your waist and pick up the spear again."

Mountain Goat took a deep breath then thrust the point of her spear into the soft yielding dirt and placed the shaft up against her thigh. Reaching behind her she felt Chamois's wrist and then followed the hand down to the club. Grasping it firmly in her hand she pulled it out of his clutch and swiftly thrust it into the belt that was around her waist and again picked up her spear.

"Do you smell that?" she asked, as Star began to squirm in her arm.

"Not only do I smell it," Chamois replied as he flared his nostrils wide, "I can taste it."

Mountain Goat opened her mouth and stuck her tongue out of her mouth just a little. She started to take in a deep breath through her mouth in order to taste the scent on the air when she glimpsed the furry outline moving through the tall grass. "Wolverine!"

161

"I knew it was a wolverine from the terrible smell." Chamois gripped his spear loosely feeling for the right balancing spot before he threw it.

"Wait!" Mountain Goat nearly shouted, as she watched the wolverine sneak through the grass. "It is tracking something."

Chamois looked to where the grass was swaying as the wolverine passed through. He knew exactly where the animal was by the parting of the grass. "It is a female," he said, as his spear moved ever so slightly in his grasp as he felt for the perfect place to hold it, before the projectile was launched toward the target.

"Are you sure; how can you be sure from this distance?"

"I can see two smaller ones trailing behind her."

"Three, there are three?" Mountain Goat asked, as she pulled Star even closer to her chest.

The Wolverine paused and glanced toward the three people and bared its fangs in defiance. The growl from deep in her throat rumbled across the open meadow. The two young wolverines trailing their mother saw her stop and heard the warning growl that grew in intensity as her sense of danger was alerted. The smaller of the two young males turned toward the men and woman and he began to growl like his mother. The larger male moved closer to his mother, and then when he saw and smelled the three people standing there began to move toward the danger.

"One of the young wolverines is coming this way." Chamois shouted, as he slowly began to turn so that he was facing the menace. "Turn toward your left and keep your back pressed firmly against mine. I will face the onslaught and protect your back."

"If my back is turned so that you are facing the wolverine, I will not be able to see it coming."

"But I will be facing it," Chamois said, as he continued to slowly turn so that he was facing directly toward the oncoming wolverine. "I will be right in front of it, if it continues with its attack."

"But I won't."

"No, but I will be the first one attacked and the first one to defend us against the skunk bear."

"Skunk bear is a good name for it. It smells!"

The young wolverine slowly advanced toward the people that were, in his mind, a threat to him. His bared his teeth and raised the hair on his back to make himself look larger and more menacing. He raised his thick bushy tail and continued to make a low growling sound deep in his throat.

"It is getting closer," Chamois said quietly. "Whatever happens, do not let your back be exposed. Keep your back right against mine."

"What about the other two? Are they also coming?"

"The mother and the other young one are squatting there looking at me. I would almost think that they were thinking about what to do. But they are not moving, at least not yet."

"Wolverines are the most vicious carnivore for their size that lives," Mountain Goat said, as she increased her grip on Star. "What if they were the size of the cave bear?"

"If they were the size of the cave bear, nothing could stand before them. They would be the most feared eater of flesh anywhere. No animal or group of hunters would be safe. Their fangs and claws would shred anything, that was caught, into pieces."

"I know, we should thank the spirits for making them only as big as they are. I have heard that they can even drive a lynx or wolf from a kill."

"That is what the tales tell," Chamois said, in a whisper as he watched the wolverine edge even closer. "They are about the size of a lynx but have no fear of lynx, fox, wolf or even hyenas."

"Can you think of what would happen if they hunted in packs like wolves?" Mountain Goat asked, as she again moved her spear ever so slightly in her hand. "A pack of them would be a terrible thing to face or defend against."

The sound of her mate's spear swishing through the air, followed a heartbeat later by the solid sound of the spear thudding into the wolverine's chest, was somehow comforting to her. The growl of pain changing to a death cry reverberated in the air.

Even as his one spear was being thrown, Chamois was shifting his other spear to his right hand. He watched his spear arch upward then curl downward, and continued to watch it until he saw it imbed itself in the wolverine's chest. As the animals scream of pain changed to its death cry, his gaze moved swiftly to the other two wolverines.

The sound of her offspring's cry seemed to make the old female react with fury. Her growl emanated from deep in her throat as she lunged toward the man. Before she had taken three leaps, the spear struck her in her neck severing the jugular. She staggered for one more step then collapsed on the ground. Her teeth were bared in a snarl of defiance and hate as she died.

"The club," Chamois shouted, as he saw the remaining wolverine lunging toward him. "Pass me the club. The female is dead but the other young one is now attacking."

Mountain Goat heard what her mate yelled but did not pass him the club. Twisting around she dropped the baby to the ground and saw the wolverine hurtling toward them as fast as his short muscular legs could carry him. Her scream matched his growl and she lunged toward him. His claws reached out for her leg as he opened his mouth wide showing his long sharp fangs.

164

Mountain Goat took one large step toward the onrushing wolverine, then lunged forward letting her weight carry her toward the animal that was attacking her and her child. Her scream came from deep within her very being. It was not a scream of fear. It was a scream of anger mixed with a little fury. Her shoulders flexed and then she drove her spear into the front of the wolverine's neck with such force that it tore through the neck and came out of the shoulder. The teeth snapped at empty air as the spear sliced the young male's windpipe, and nicked the jugular before shattering the shoulder blade as it exited the shoulder.

Chamois looked at the wolverines, then at his mate. Shaking his head he slowly relaxed as he realized that the immediate danger was now ended. "It is over," he said in a whisper. "But I think we should get our spears and leave here before any other animals come to the scent of the dead."

"Not until I skin these wolverines. The hair of a wolverine is the best for hoods and covering the face. Snow and frost will not stick and clump to the hairs. If any snow or frost does stick you can brush it off easily. There are three of them and three of us. It seems as if the spirits made their path and our path meet here so that we could kill them for the fur." Mountain Goat knelt down by the large female and slowly began to gut and skin her.

Chamois pulled his spears out of the two wolverines that he had killed then retrieved his mate's spear from the one she had killed. He studied the shafts to see if they had been damaged. He turned the spears slowly in his hands as he carefully looked for a crack in the shaft. He looked at the finely made flint points to see if they had been broken or chipped. "Your blade has a chip out of it. It must have been damaged when it hit the shoulder blade. It is not too bad, I think I can reshape it without having to completely replace the point."

Without even bothering to look up from where her skinning blade was cutting through the thick hide, Mountain Goat shook her head from side to side. "Replace it! We have many new spear points in the traveling packs. Why work on an old point when we have new ones? Just unwrap the shaft from the point and put on a new point. Then you can help me finish these hides."

Star walked over to where they were and grabbed her nose. "They stink." Then she held out her arms to her mother. "Pick up."

"I have her," Chamois said, as he picked her up.

"Dada hold Star," the little girl said, as she snuggled closer to the large man.

"Yes, little one," he whispered gently, as he kissed her. "Your Dada has you and will hold you while your mother skins the wolverines."

"You could take her and continue to look for more sign of the megaloceros. I would like to see one of them alive and not just the antlers. It would be a sight that would stay in our memories for as long as we are alive."

"It would be a sight, you are right about that."

"What are you trying to say?"

"I would not want to hunt any animal that large with just two hunters. The danger is too much."

"Is it anymore dangerous than just a man, a woman and a child traveling alone trying to follow a trail that is moons old?"

"There is a difference," he replied, "between a danger that happens and a danger that you try to find. This danger, the wolverines that our path and their path met here, was not planned. It just happened. The spirits made our path and their path cross here. But I do not want to go looking for danger. We have to think about Star."

"You are right. I would not want to put Star in danger."

"Star, would you like to help Dada look for something to eat?"

"Eat?"

"I think that I saw some berry bushes back there just before the wolverines came. You like berries don't you?"

"I like the black ones; are there black ones?"

"Only the spirits know what color they are until we find them. Then we will know what the spirits know."

"Chamois, I do not like that talk."

"What talk?"

"Saying we will know what the spirits know. No one knows what the spirits know. They know everything. We do not. That is why they are the spirits who guard us; why they are the spirits who let us learn what they want us to learn. We are like babies that they watch over."

"I was just saying that the spirits know the color of the berries before we find them. That they know before we know."

"It is still not a good thing to say. Please do not talk like that."

"Dada, I want to eat some berries."

"Are you sure that you want us to go off and leave you here?"

"GO! I am fine here. I still have one more wolverine to finish skinning before I can begin to work on the skins and make them into parkas."

"Keep a spear close and yell if you see or smell anything."

"Don't worry about me, I will be careful. Star wants the berries you told her about."

"She always wants to eat. But we will go and search for the berry patch. I hope that there are enough for her. She would eat berries until her belly sticks out."

"She does like to eat, that is certain. Now will you go and let me finish skinning these animals and making the skins into parkas?"

Chamois looked at his mate, then the young girl standing there fidgeting waiting for him to take her berry picking. "It is getting too dark. We will do it in the morning."

"NO!" Star screamed and started crying. "You said you would take me to find berries."

The eerie hooting of an owl made the young girl stop and glance up into the night sky. The one hoot was followed by another and then another.

In the distance, the howling of a hunting wolf rent the gathering darkness. Soon the air was full of the cries of the pack on the hunt.

"No berry picking for us," Chamois said, as he began to gather wood for a fire. "Listen to the hunters out there. They are telling us that soon it will be dark. That they are getting ready to start their hunts. I want at least two fires blazing before it is so dark that we cannot see what is slinking around."

Star shivered as yet another cry tore through the night air. She moved closer to her mother and father for comfort and protection. "I will help make fire," she said, as she began picking up twigs and small branches.

12

"I think that we had better make camp," Fox said, as he stumbled and nearly fell over a log that was sticking out into the path. "If we keep going in the darkness, someone is going to get hurt."

"You may be right," Ibex said, as she motioned the rest to stop. "It is getting too dark to see more than a few steps in front of where we are walking. There could be a hole or something in the trail, and a broken leg is not what I want to have happen."

Moon patted her growing belly and slumped to the ground. "Thank the spirits," she muttered, more to herself than anyone around her. "This baby in my belly is making it harder and harder to keep up with the clan during these treks."

"I heard that," Marmot said, as she plopped down on the ground next to Moon. "And I agree. I should be having this baby in about one more moon and the travel over these mountains is hard."

"Winter is coming soon, I can feel the chill in the air, especially at night." Moon said, as she began to unroll her sleeping skins.

Woolly Rhino glanced over to where his mate was talking to Marmot. "We will have the shelter up before it gets too dark."

Gesher and the other men were spreading the thick hides out on the ground along with the poles that held the skins. The large traveling shelter was something completely unknown to them until their meeting with the Danub Clan three moons ago. When they saw the way that the Danub Clan was able to put up a shelter so quickly, Gesher and Wolf had begged for the secret of the traveling shelter.

Horse, the leader of the hunting party from the Danub Clan had refused to show them the way the poles were made and attached to the hides to make the shelter.

But after Ibex, along with Woolly Rhino and Fox had sat at the campfire of the Danub Clan until the morning sun began to illuminate the eastern horizon, Horse had relented and agreed to show them the secret. But he had wanted much in return.

The Clan of Ibex had given them 15 of their best spear points; 4 of the points with the backward pointing barb, 10 spear shafts and nearly half of all their meat. But Ibex had said that it was a good trade. She and Horse had promised to welcome any member of either clan to their campfires. Their handclasp of friendship was binding on all members of both clans.

The hunting party from the Danub Clan had spent two days with Gesher and the men showing them the way to make the poles and to attach the hides to the shelter so that it could be put up and taken down without damage to the poles or the covering hides.

"There, it's up." Gesher said, as he bent over and went inside.

Moon rose from where she was sprawled out on the ground, and taking her sleeping skins, followed Gesher and the others inside.

Rabbit was squatting in the middle of the shelter twirling the twirling stick against the platform. "I could use some help," she said, without taking her eyes off the platform.

"I'll help," Woolly Rhino said, as he sat down next to Rabbit. "You keep twirling the stick as your hands slide down the stick. When they are close to the bottom, I will start at the top and make sure that my hands are moving like your hands. Then when my hands are close to the bottom, you can start at the top."

"I know how to do it, Rabbit said with just a little anger or perhaps annoyance in her voice. "You don't have to tell me how to have two people work together to make a fire."

170

"Of course you do," he replied. "I was just trying to use these few heartbeats when everyone is gathered inside the shelter to help explain to Ox and Badger how it is done. They are starting to notice what we do. Watching what men and women do is the best way to learn."

"You're right. They are getting old enough to begin to learn. I have seen Ox sitting quietly, watching the men make spears or make points for the spears."

"So has Badger. He has begun to look at stones."

"For points?"

"I haven't asked him, but that is what I think he is doing."

Ibex and Fawn sat down and started to prepare the meal that the clan would be eating that night. Fawn took a flaming branch from the fire that Rabbit and Woolly Rhino had started and placed it under the pile of branches and twigs that they had prepared.

As the pile of branches and twigs ignited, they spread the burning coals into a circle and then added more wood. Ibex took the two thick oak sidepieces, shaped like a **Y** and thrust them into the ground on both sides of the fire. Fawn took the long thin pole that they had poked though the hunk of bison thigh and placed it on the two **Y** shaped sidepieces. The pole extended out from the two Y shaped sidepieces, about a span of two hands.

As the meat slowly cooked over the bed of hot coals and burning wood, Fawn or Ibex, would take hold of the pole, holding the meat by the edge that stuck out beyond the fire, and turn it. They turned it slowly so that the thick juicy meat was seared all around. The sizzling sounds, from the cooking meat as it dripped small amounts of juice onto the fire, made most of the talking stop and brought everyone closer to the fire.

"That fresh bison smells good," Badger exclaimed, as he edged even closer to the fire.

"Careful," his mother said, as she grabbed him and pulled him back away from the flames. "Don't let your stomach chase away your caution. Fire burns!"

"It burns the wood and it could burn you," Lynx, said as he motioned to his mate and son to move closer to where he was sitting. "Wait for the meat to be finished. Or do you want to eat cold meat?"

"No," Badger said, as he settled down next to his father and mother. "I like it as hot as it can be."

"Our supply of skins for clothing is nearly gone," Fox said, as he sat munching a large slice of bison. "I need some new foot coverings, and we need more covers to keep the chill of the night away from our sleeping area."

"Yes, we do," Ibex answered, as she sliced another hunk of meat of the roasted bison thigh. "We should plan on staying here for a moon, perhaps a little longer, while we replenish our supplies."

"And until the babies are born," Gesher added, as he glanced over to where Marmot and Moon were sitting with their mates.

The first early morning rays from the Sun Spirit were just beginning to illuminate the horizon when the hunting party left to start the hunt. Wolf was the first in line and quickly increased the speed that they were walking. His eyes swept back and forth as he watched the trail in front of the hunters and out to the sides for any approaching danger. Any predator that could be lurking in front of them had to be seen by him so that he could alert them to the danger and the group could react. If he saw any animals that could be hunted for food, he had to identify them and signal those behind him of what they were, how many there were, what direction they were going and if there were any other animals around that could spook and scare them before the hunters could close in for the kill.

At the very end of the line of hunters, walked Woolly Rhino. He was the one watching the back trail. He took a few steps, then paused as he swiveled around to see if anything was following them. The danger of a massive cave lion, pack of wolves, bears, lynx, wolverine or other carnivore picking up their scent trail and following them was constant. Just as they were looking to come upon a trail made by anything they could hunt, the predators did the same thing. If any carnivore, large or small, found the fresh scent of anything they knew was within their ability to hunt down and kill, they would follow the scent until the prey was located. Then they would move in closer without making any sound until they were close enough to leap to the attack. It was his responsibility to protect the hunters from any attack being launched from behind them

Woolly Rhino nervously kept glancing back down their back trail. Then he would look ahead to where the rest of the hunters were. He was the first person that any carnivore would attack if it picked up their scent trail and stalked them. But he also had to protect the rest of the hunters from any attack on their backs. They were concentrating on what was in front of them or to the sides. Prey animals were what they were searching for. He was the only one who was intent on watching for danger.

Wolf increased the pace even more. He wanted to get as far away from the campsite as he could before he started to hunt seriously. The wind had been blowing furiously all night, and the smoke from their fires had wafted on the wind for quite a long distance. He was still picking up a faint smell of smoke even now when he inhaled deeply. Some of the animals, not all, but many were alerted by the scent of smoke and would leave the area. Smoke usually meant fire, and fire was death coming on the wind. If an animal could not flee the flames and smoke by running away from the fire, or scurry into a deep burrow far under ground, they would die in the fire.

Woolly Rhino saw the hunters in front of him begin to walk even faster. He started to walk even faster to keep up. He would almost run a spear throw until he was almost touching the back of the man in front of him, then stop for 10 to 15 heartbeats to carefully survey the area in back of them. He watched the grasses to see if they were moving in a pattern that would indicate that an animal was sneaking though the tall waving grass. He listened for any rustling of fallen leaves or a cracking of the smallest of twigs. He flared his nostrils wide trying to smell any scents on the moving air currents.

Wolf suddenly halted and signaled stop. Every hunter, except for Woolly Rhino froze in place. Not a foot moved as each man and woman in the hunting party concentrated on watching Wolf for more signs. Woolly Rhino was intently watching the back trail when the signal to stop was given. He failed to see the first sign or even the second sign. But as he turned to again resume the track that the hunters in front of him were on, he saw them beginning to move outward and away from the trail.

Woolly Rhino nearly ran to catch up to the hunters that were moving extremely silently toward the open pasture where the auroch were congregated. He had taken two steps before he realized that the others were creeping toward the massive animals. He took in a deep breath and then dropped to his knees in order to crawl toward the auroch and the other hunters. He paused for a few heartbeats to gather the droppings of the auroch and rub himself with their dung to hide his scent. He had not seen the other hunters do it, he had been watching the back trail, but he knew that they had also covered themselves with the animal dung. Using the dung from the animals that they were hunting completely masked the scent of the hunters, so that they could get close enough to their prey to successfully launch their spears.

The auroch herd was meandering around as they grazed on the lush tall vegetation. Every few heartbeats, one or more of the massive animals would look around before again grazing. The herd bulls however, seemed to be a little agitated. They would forage for a few heartbeats then raise their heads and bellow. It was mating season and the mature bulls were vying for dominance, and the privilege of being the bull, to mate with the cows as they came into their breeding cycle.

174

Periodically, two of the large bulls would stare at each other for many heartbeats, and then bellowing as loudly as they could charge toward each other. The resulting clash of horn, on horn as one of the massive animals struck the other, was impressive. The two antagonists would, as soon as contact was made, begin to thrust mightily against each other. The deep resonating bellowing would increase as the two fighting males pushed and shoved trying to gain an advantage over their opponent. Hooves would send the dirt flying as they pawed the ground attempting to get their feet planted firmly so that they could push the other bull backward.

The cows and young males and females would move away from the scene of combat and continue to graze, only periodically lifting their heads for a heartbeat or two to stare at the two sweating straining bulling vying for dominance, and the right to mate with the cows that were ready to breed.

Suddenly one of the fighting males would break away from the battle and turn and run. The victorious male would chase the vanquished bull for a short distance, then turn and return to the cow that he wanted to mate. The battles were occurring all over the pasture as the many adult males continued their fights for breeding rights to the hundreds of females in the herd. Sometimes, as many as five or more clashes were occurring at the same time.

Gesher sent a silent signal to the hunters that were slowly advancing on the large herd of auroch. The signs were seen and relayed to the other hunters by those closest to Gesher. The silent sign conveyed his thankfulness over the breeding noise covering up any accidental sound that the hunters may make.

Wolf, who had been named the hunt leader, squatted silently as he sent hand signals and used body movements to position his hunters in an arc around the herd. When he was satisfied that all of the men and woman in his hunting party were positioned exactly as he wanted them he sent out the sign that they should drop to their bellies and crawl as close to a specific animal as they dared.

Wolf began to slither slowly forward on his stomach. As he drew closer and closer to the large female he had selected, he paused and inhaled deeply three times. He didn't dare get any closer to the herd. Just as he was about to give the signal to the hunters to start the assault on the herd, a young bull began to stare right at him. It pawed the ground twice and snorted, trying to clear its nostrils and catch a scent of whatever it was that was sprawled in front of him on the ground. But all the young bull could smell was auroch droppings. He snorted once again, and then began to graze.

As the young male turned away from his hiding place in the tall waving grasses, Wolf sent forth the signal to begin the attack on the herd. He opened his mouth just a little, and sent forth the sign. His cry was a perfect imitation of the scream of an eagle.

As the cry sounded, eight hunters rose nearly as one and launched a spear. Within just one heartbeat eight spears were hurtling through the air toward their targets. The sight of the eight hunters, suddenly standing up nearly within the outer edges of the milling heard, added to the bellowing of the eight animals that the hunters had selected, as the spears thudded into their massive chest regions sent the animals into a panic.

Within a heartbeat, the whole herd began a stampede toward an area that they considered safe. But before the panic-stricken bovines could reach a safe distance, more spears flew though the air. The hunters had sent their second spears racing after the fleeing animals. A few of the hunters had even managed to launch a third spear. As the spears penetrated the thick hides of the second group of auroch they began bellowing even louder.

Gesher breathed a sigh of relief as he watched the way the herd had bolted. Wolf had done a good job of positioning the hunters in an arc that allowed them to nearly surround the herd, but left them one side for an escape. The side that he selected for them to run, without having any hunters exposed to danger, had been the very route the animals had run. The herd thundered across the open pasture and into the scrub brush at the edge of the clearing.

Behind the herd, 15 animals struggled to keep up with the rest of the animals as they disappeared into the brush and trees. Three others had already fallen to the ground.

Fox gingerly approached one of the animals that he had speared. He saw the eye closest to him slowly follow him as he walked closer. He was about three steps from the young bull when it took one long look at him and began to struggle to its feet. It opened its mouth to bellow a challenge, but all that came out of the bull's mouth was a combination of saliva, blood and other fluids. Lurching to its front feet, the young bull swept his horns in a circle trying to catch the hunter with his long curving horns. But he was not able to rise completely because his back legs were unable to support his weight. The spear that was imbedded in his lungs had nicked the major nerves that controlled the back legs as it plunged into the bull. Fox sprung out of the way of the swinging head and deadly horns, then lunged forward and drove his third and final spear into the neck of the bull severing the larynx. The bull rolled his eyes as the supply of oxygen to his brain was suddenly ended, and he slumped slowly onto the ground.

Ibex watched her second auroch stagger and fall. Its bellow reverberated across the pasture. Ibex carefully felt along the shaft of her third spear until she knew by the balance in her hand that it was poised to throw. She drew in a deep breath and threw it as hard as she could. The distance was short and it flew straight toward the prone animal. It hit with a resounding thunk and buried itself halfway up the shaft of the spear.

Lynx was bent over the large cow that he had killed with his first spear but was watching the staggering path of the second auroch that he had speared as the massive bull tried to escape the encircling hunters. He sent a silent prayer of thanks to the spirits as he saw it fall, regain its feet wobble another few paces, then fall again. It bellowed once, then was still.

Fox glanced over to where Woolly Rhino was squatting over one of his kills. "Do you think our mates are alright? I still think that

177

one of us should have stayed behind with the two women who are expecting."

"Moon said for us to go, that she and Marmot would be fine. I heard your mate tell you the same. Besides, the fresh skins will make the best clothes for all of us, even the newborns, when they are born. The hair on these auroch is course and thick to protect them from the cold winter winds and snows. If it protects the auroch so good, it will protect us."

"I can't help it. I worry that something will happen. We all came hunting leaving just the two women and the children back at the camp. If one of them starts to have a baby what will happen?"

"Well then, the faster we skin and butcher these animals, the faster we can all start back to the camp."

Fawn smiled at the banter that was happening between the two men whose mates were expecting. When she saw Ibex glance her way, she sent a slight but very meaningful series of signs to the leader of their clan. She mouthed the words as she sent the signals. "Can you believe the way these two are behaving? You would think that they were the first men whose mates were expecting."

"They are as nervous as a lone hunter that hears the cry of a pack of wolves on a track."

"That would make anyone a little nervous, but both have been in camp when a woman was giving birth."

"You're right, by their tenth spring, all boys and girls have heard and seen babies born. Could it be that they are very young?"

"Perhaps, but they are right about one thing. The faster we skin and butcher these animals, the quicker we will be safely back in camp. With all the blood and guts from these auroch that we killed on the ground, it will not be long before the scavengers start to show up. And with the scavengers come the predators looking for a kill that they do not have to kill."

Fox looked up from where he was slicing the back haunches of the large cow into smaller sections so that they could be taken back to camp. "If anyone is finished skinning and butchering their animals, start cutting down some large limbs off the trees so that we can use them to carry the meat and skins back to the camp."

"I am nearly done," Ibex said, as she stood up and stretched her back. She placed her hands on the small of her back and arched backward as she twisted her upper body. She heard quite a few small snaps and cracks as she manipulated herself to relieve some of the aches and pains she felt. "There are quite a few branches and limbs that should be just about right to use to make a drag along for the meat and skins."

13

"I felt a twinge," Moon suddenly said. "No, it is more than a twinge; it is a birthing pain."

"Are you sure," Marmot said, glancing over to where her friend sat by the fire. "I have been getting little pains but they are not like the pains that the other women talked about."

"I heard them also. Ibex told me about them and what to expect, and so did the other women who have had babies. But I think that these are birthing pains."

"But it is too soon. Our babies are not yet ready to be born. It has not been ten moons."

"Babies come when they want to be born. The spirits call to the baby and tell it that it must be born now. I have heard of some women who give birth as soon as seven moons."

"And some take eleven moons before they have the baby, but most are born after the Moon Spirit shows her full face ten times." Marmot suddenly stood up and placed her hands over her belly. "You may be right, I felt the baby drop way down in my belly and my back is really starting to hurt. That sign, the dropping way down and the backache is a sign that all the females who have had babies talk about."

Moon picked up a handful of small branches and threw them on the fire. "I am going to go and bring back more limbs and branches for the fire. I think I will even start a second fire. It is nearly dark, and with just the two of us here along with the young children, I want to make sure that we have enough wood to last the night and fire to keep away any predators that may be prowling around searching for easy prey."

"It is getting dark, and the hunters are not back. They said that they would be returning by the time it got dark. I don't know if I want to be here with the children in the dark without a man here to protect us." Marmot said, as she stood up and looked into the gathering darkness that was creeping closer and closer to their campfires.

"I can't believe that you said that!" Moon exclaimed. "You are a female of The Chosen by birth. I am a female of The Chosen by birth. We are not afraid of anything that walks or crawls or flies. I have seen you on the hunt, you face the charge without fear."

Marmot stood there looking at Moon for a few heartbeats before turning away and sending signs to Badger and Ox. "Boys," she called as she sent them exaggerated signs and signals to get their attention. "It is getting dark and you have to come closer to the fire. I heard a hyena coughing in the distance and the darkness holds many dangers." When she saw the two young boys walking slowly back to the campfire, she sighed and rotated her shoulders to release some of the strain.

"What was that?"

"I don't know, but it sounded big and the noise was very close."

Badger and Ox heard the loud crack of the limb breaking and broke into a fast run. They knew how far away from the safety, or at least the supposed safety, of the large fire blazing back at their camp they were. The two young boys raced over the ground, leaping small rocks and boulders. Another snapping of a branch lent urgency to their flight toward the two women standing next to the fire.

"Something big is out there and I can't see anything." Marmot said as she peered into the gathering darkness. For a heartbeat she glanced up into the night sky before again concentrating her attention toward the two boys running toward her and whatever it was that broke the silence of the night with the breaking sound of branches, or perhaps limbs. "Can you see anything?"

"Nothing," Moon replied as she balanced her spear in her hand. "I can't see anything out there that doesn't seem to belong out there. But you should get a spear, perhaps two, and be ready if there is something stalking us or the boys."

"Yes, I should," Marmot said, as she bent over and picked up two spears and a small club. Sticking the club into her belt she gripped one spear loosely in her throwing hand and carried the other one in the jabbing position in her other hand.

The two boys jumped the large boulder and collapsed on the ground by the roaring fire. "What was that?" Ox asked, as he rolled over and looked up at Moon. "It sounded like a mammoth or something big like that."

"Maybe it was a cave lion creeping close enough to leap on you and swallow you in one big bite," Badger started to say, but the last few words were so mixed with laughter that he could hardly say all of them.

"Enough," Moon scolded, as she glared at the boy. "There is something out there, and it could be a cave lion. What if it really is something so dangerous that it attacks and kills all of us?"

Badger looked up at the woman and opened his mouth as if to say something when another snapping of a limb, so close to where they were standing, alerted them and made all of their heads turn toward the sound. "That was close," Badger whispered, as he edged closer to Moon.

"I can't see anything!" Marmot exclaimed in frustration, as she fidgeted with her spear. She adjusted her grip yet again on the shaft of the weapon. A slight moan escaped from between her lips as she felt the pain shoot through her belly. "Please spirits," she whispered under her breath, "not now, please not now. Do not call to the baby in my belly to be born now."

"Badger," Moon said as she reached for a spear and handed it to him. "Take this spear. I know it is big and you can hardly hold it, but take it and use it if you have to. Pretend that you are trying to stick a piece of meat onto the tip of a wooden shaft to cook over the fire. Jab and jab and jab." She paused and then did the same for Ox. "Stay close to us."

Ox took the spear that was given to him and gripped it as tightly as he could. His two hands held it so hard that his knuckles started to turn white from the strain. Suddenly he knew. They were in danger, not just a little danger, but a danger so bad that the two women were worried. He knew they were worried when they gave the spears to him and Badger. He heard the concern in their voices and saw it on their faces.

Badger also saw and heard the anxiety that the women showed when they whispered to each other, and on their faces in the gloom of the night. He looked at the spear that was handed to him and knew! He and Ox along with the two women could be with the spirits before the Sun Spirit woke in the morning.

"Back to back," Moon whispered to Marmot. "I think that we should try to defend ourselves by standing back to back so that nothing can jump us from behind."

"But the boys, what about the boys?" Marmot asked, as she took a heartbeat or two to glance toward where the two young boys were huddled by their feet.

"Stay between our feet," Moon said to Badger and Ox. "No matter what happens, stay between our feet. Do not move from between our feet."

"I won't" Badger said, as he squatted down with his spear clasped tightly in his hands.

"I won't move no matter what happens," Ox whispered, as he knelt with his spear gripped as tight as he could next to the comfort of the women's legs.

A pain raced down and through the belly of Moon as she peered into the darkness. It was sharp and lasted for many heartbeats. "Marmot," Moon whispered quietly to her friend. "The birthing pains are starting to become very close together. I think that the spirits are telling the baby in my belly that they want him, or maybe her, to be born now."

"Hush," Marmot replied. "I am having pains also, but I am asking the spirits to wait until the danger passes before the baby comes. I am asking and asking and also asking for the hunters to return quickly. You should too."

Before Moon could answer, another contraction raked her making her wince and then gasp. "I don't think that I can."

"But," Marmot started to say, when she saw Moon grab her belly and slowly sink to her knees.

Badger looked up at Moon and saw her crumble to her knees. He felt the fear slowly growing in his belly. Something was out there; something dangerous was stalking though the grass and brush that surrounded their campfires. Now, one of the two females, who were left behind to guard them, was moaning in pain and no longer was standing guard.

"If only the Moon Spirit was awake and looking down on us," Marmot said, as she continued to slowly swivel her head back and forth trying to see as much as possible around their sanctuary. "But she is still sleeping even though the night is dark and her children are awake."

"The baby is coming now, I can feel it pushing its way out of my belly." Moon moaned as her contractions continued to force the baby out of her belly.

184

Ox saw the pain on the woman's face and heard what she was saying. He was young, not even five birthing seasons, or springs in age, but he knew about babies. "Lean on me," he told the struggling woman. "I will hold you like your mate would if he was here."

"You're just a boy," she gasped as more pains tore through her.

"I am big enough!" Ox said as he grabbed her tightly. "You need someone to hold onto as the baby comes. You need someone to help keep you standing as the baby is born. Now lean on me."

"Do it," Marmot said under her breath as she strained to see anything in the gloom of the darkness. "If Ox says he is big enough, then he is. Maybe Badger can help a little. I can't!"

Moon groaned as another pain tore through her belly. The sound of her moaning seemed to stir a response from whatever it was that was slowly circling their encampment. A series of growls and snarls emanated from the darkness just beyond their sight. The glow from their campfires illuminated a large area, but only allowed them to see what was within the area. Beyond the opening where they were huddled, the darkness hid everything. Without the glow from the moon, all they had to help them see past the places that the fires lit up was the very faint light from the stars shinning overhead. But even these were not enough as the constantly moving clouds drifted by, and for many heartbeats obscured many of the stars and the meager light that they afforded.

Ox gripped Moon tightly even as he continued to search the surrounding vegetation for any movement that could be the beginning of an attack, by whatever it was that was prowling around their campsite. Suddenly he heard her moan end in what could have been a sob, or perhaps a cry. Then the baby nearly plopped onto the rough ground, but instead was caught by Badger and gently lowered to the earth.

Moon gasped once more then looked down between her legs at the tiny bundle curled up on the ground where Badger had placed her.

"The spirits have given me a baby girl," she exclaimed as she sat down next to Badger and Ox. "Cut the tube, the tube has to be cut."

Ox looked up at the woman. "I have no knife."

"Here catch this one," Marmot whispered.

Ox saw the thin knife leave Marmot's hand but missed it as it tried to catch it. "Badger pick it up."

Badger crawled to where the knife was hidden in the grass and picked it up. He started to hand it to Ox when he saw the eyes in the grass starring right at him. They were large and green and looking right at him. He started to scream then stopped. He was a male of The Chosen and males of The Chosen did not scream in fright. They faced whatever danger faced them and lived or died as men. He sucked in a breath then tried to say as calmly as he could. "There is a big cat crawling right toward me."

"The birthing smell must be attracting it!" Marmot yelled.

Moon struggled back up to her feet as she cradled her newborn baby daughter to her breast. "Where is it?"

"Right in front of me!" Badger yelled, as he scurried backward toward the safety of the legs of the two women.

Screaming in fury the large predator gathered its legs under itself and hurtled toward the woman and baby. The smell of the birth still lingered on the night air. His hunting scream was answered by the screams of the women.

Moon screamed her defiance toward the onrushing carnivore and threw her spear toward the gaping jaws.

Marmot's spear left her hand just as her yell of warning erupted from her mouth.

The terrible one felt the spear from Moon glance off his shoulder, leaving a long thin gash that immediately began to ooze blood. The spear that Marmot threw sliced the side of his neck but did not penetrate enough to cause serious bleeding or injury. But the flaming branch thrust into his mouth by Ox seared his mouth and tongue. The flames and heat, that were trapped for the briefest of a heartbeat inside his wide-open mouth, burnt the inside skin of his cheeks and lips, as Ox shoved the flaming branch toward the charging killer.

The terrible one twisted around in one swift movement as he shook his head to get rid of the burning sensation in his mouth. He leapt high in the air, as he turned backward in one fluid movement shaking his head rapidly back and forth.

His shriek of pain from the burning sensation in his mouth was suddenly replaced by a death cry, as the spears tore into him. Three spears thudded into his right side as two others buried themselves in his left side.

Woolly Rhino burst through the tangle of brush and small trees that made up the perimeter of the encampment. He was followed one heartbeat later by Fox and Ibex. "Are you alright?" he yelled, as he yanked his spear out of the terrible one. "We heard you yelling and we rushed back. The others are coming with the meat and skins."

Fox paused for a heartbeat, looking at the dead carnivore stretched out on the ground, then wrapped his arms around his mate. "We heard you and threw our loads on the ground and ran all the way back. It is good that the spirits let your voices reach our ears so that we could get here just as the terrible one attacked. I saw what Ox did; he was very brave."

Ibex paused at the body and looked at it. She just stood there staring at the large killer. "Whose spears are these? We threw three spears but there are five spears in him."

The voice from the darkness made her turn. "They are our spears. We heard the voices of the women and boys calling and the spirits brought us here. We saw the great killer; we knew what it was even though we have never seen one. They are the killer of all killers. Now we have seen one and helped kill one."

Fox heard the voices and tried to see who was talking. "Come closer to the fire," he said, into the pitch-black darkness. "The other hunters will be here in a few more heartbeats with enough meat to feed all of us for many moons."

Three forms slowly materialized out of the darkness. "I am called Chamois, and this is my mate Mountain Goat and our daughter Star. We have been traveling for many moons, seeking a clan that calls itself the Clan of Ibex."

Fox looked at Ibex and saw the grin on her face. Then he saw the slight movement of her hands as she sent a hidden sign to the others gathered around the campfire. He nodded and then turned to the three people advancing toward them. "Why would you go looking for a clan? There are many clans and bands around here. The hunting is good; the water is cold and flows clean. One clan is like another, isn't it?"

"Perhaps, but if you ever meet people from the Clan of Ibex you will know why we are seeking them." Chamois paused and then took Star's hand as he pulled her onto his lap by the fire. "The leader of the clan is a woman. She and her mate Gesher have been the leaders of the clan since it was started. They were the first two people in the clan."

"The first two, how is that possible? Clans have existed for as long as the memories have existed. The clans are forever." Marmot added, with a gleam in her eye that only a few saw.

Chamois was about to say something when his eyes saw the people that were standing there. His head tilted slightly as he looked carefully at the men and women gathered around him and his mate and daughter. His elbow nudged Mountain Goat and he leaned

188

over and whispered in her ear. "Look at these people. Look very carefully at the males. They are big and robust like all men of The Chosen, but they talk like men of The Second People."

Mountain Goat paused as she slowly ran her fingers through the hair of her daughter. "They are muscular, but all the people of The Chosen that we have seen look that way. They use words and signs that The Second People use, but they may have traded with a band or two of The Second People." She whispered back bending her head close to that of her mate. "Since we started our search looking for the Clan of Ibex, we have found two clans of The Chosen and one band of The Second People. All three were willing to trade with us and welcomed us to their campfires."

"Yes, that is true." Chamois said, "but" He never had a chance to say more because suddenly the small clearing was filled with men and women dragging piles of meat and skins on poles that were tied together.

"Is everyone safe?" Gesher shouted, as he saw the terrible one stretched out on the ground.

"What happened?" Rabbit exclaimed, looking at Moon.

"We heard noises as it got darker and darker. Then I started to have the baby. The noises grew louder and came closer as the pains got worse. Just as I had the baby, Ox saw the terrible one creeping up on us. We fought it as good as we could. If the others had not gotten here just as they did, I fear that all of us would be going to live with the sprits by this heartbeat."

Marmot suddenly fell to the ground moaning. "My baby is coming, I can feel it pushing to get out."

Ibex pushed through the people that were standing around Moon and Marmot. "I wasn't here when Moon had her baby. But I can see that she and the little girl are fine. How are you doing?" she asked as she squatted next to Marmot.

"I'm not sure," the young woman replied, as she struggled to get into the birthing position.

Chamois looked at Mountain Goat and shook his head from side to side. "They are the ones, these are the Clan of Ibex. We have found them! But why were they saying what they said?"

Mountain Goat smiled at her mate. "I think I know. Remember how they were when they came to our camp to help our band when we camped by the water that was bad? After they had made sure that we were not all dying from the poison in the water, and after they brought us fresh meat, they laughed and made jokes with each other. They teased the members of their clan and also started to tease some of our people. I think that they were teasing us."

"Gesher," Ibex said, as she knelt next to Marmot, "I could use some help."

Gesher spun around from where he was talking to Fox and his eyebrows arched upward. "What is it?"

"I think that there is a problem with Marmot's birthing. She is in position, the pains are constant, but the baby is not coming."

"Do you need some Fenigreek to induce the birthing?"

"Yes, Fenigreek is needed so that she can have the baby."

Fox looked at his mate, then at Ibex and Gesher. "What's wrong? Is something the matter with Marmot? Is something wrong with the baby? Do something!"

Lynx saw his mother and father sitting on the ground next to the straining woman and heard what was being said. Sending a series of fast signs to the members of his clan, he tapped Fox on the shoulder. "Come with me, we have to finish the animals we brought back from the hunt. The skins need to be prepared to be made into clothing. The meat has to be cut into strips so that it can

190

be smoked. The stomachs have to be cleaned for water carriers. There is a lot of work to be done and it is already very dark."

Fawn grabbed his hand as she tried to get him to go with her. "Help me drag the carcass of the terrible one away from here. I don't like to have it so close to the children. Ox and Badger were very brave in helping kill the terrible one, but I want to get it away from them now that it is dead. I am also worried that the stench and blood will attract other carnivores. There may even be another one of those killers lurking around here."

"But I want to be here with Marmot," Fox said, as he pulled free from her grasp. "I thought that one of the traditions of the Clan of Ibex was that the men stayed and helped with the birthing. She needs me to hold her. I have to be there for her to lean on as the baby comes."

"Let him stay," Ibex said quietly, as she felt the bulging belly of Marmot. "The spirits may be calling her soon. I am worried."

Fox's eyes widened in disbelief as he heard what Ibex was saying. Was there something that wrong with the birth? Could his mate really die? "Do something!" He shouted so loudly that every head turned toward where he was standing. "We have been mates for only a few seasons. This is the first baby she has had in her belly. Do something!"

Gesher looked up from where he and Ibex were trying to help Marmot. "I think that Nepeta and also Bee Balm is needed. Both help someone to relax. She is scared and holding back with her pushing. We need to give her something to make her less nervous and more relaxed."

Fawn squatted next to the three people and rubbed the belly of Marmot. "It is hard, very hard and I don't know if I can feel the baby moving. What about using Humulus?"

"Humulus is more of a medicine to make someone sleep," Gesher said. "But keep thinking like that. A medicine woman needs to be thinking of all the plants we use and what is the best one, or two or even more, to use. We need to get her to relax, to stop clenching her muscles. Humulus would probably make her sleep and she must be awake to have the baby. But start making the Nepeta and Bee Balm for her. That would help."

"Here drink this," Ibex said to Marmot. "Drink all of it as quickly as you can. Then stop squatting and lay down."

"Lay down?" Gesher asked as he glanced up at his mate. "Women give birth kneeling or squatting, so that the baby comes out and the male of the hearth catches it, and holds it as he gives it the breath of life. You want her to lay down?"

"Yes, I do!" Ibex said. "Marmot listen to me. Lay down on your back and pull your knees up toward your belly. Relax, close your eyes and think of your mate. Think of Fox and how much you love him. Think of the baby you are going to have and how much you will love the baby as he or she suckles at your breast."

"I see the baby's head, it is coming," Gesher said, as he sat by Marmot's knees. "There is no hair on its head."

"Push," Ibex and Fawn said, nearly at the same heartbeat.

Marmot reached up and grabbed Fox's hand and squeezed as hard as she could. Her face started to turn as white as Gesher's face. Then with a scream so loud that it silenced the sounds of the night birds, Marmot pushed the baby from her belly.

"A baby girl, it's a baby girl," Gesher said, as he handed the little one to Fox. "Careful of the head, you have to support it with your hand. And you have to give her the breath of life."

"I only have one arm, I am afraid that I will drop her."

"One arm is enough to hold a baby close to your chest so that the baby can hear the beating of your heart. But I will give her the

192

breath of life, that does take two hands," Gesher said, as he lifted the tiny form to his mouth.

"Wait," Marmot said, reaching up toward the baby. "Please let me do it."

"You have had a hard birth," Ibex told her. "You should get some sleep. I saw how hard you fought not to have the baby. Then you fought to have the baby. It is not good to be afraid of birth. The spirits have made females special. Males do not give birth, males do not suckle the newborns and the babies. Only women have been made by the spirits to have and to feed babies. You should sleep now to get your strength back."

"No, I want to hold her as I give her life," Marmot said, as she took the baby from Gesher.

The baby's first gasp and then cry made her smile. "Now I will rest, and Fox can hold the baby as she listens to the beating of his heart," Marmot said, handing the little girl to her mate.

Ibex motioned to Gesher and Fawn. Then walked slowly away from where Fox and Marmot were stretched out on the ground. "She has lost a lot of blood. I have never seen anyone bleed so much having a baby. We have to get her to take the medicine that stops bleeding. I have a lot of Verbena we can use that. How is our supply of Bloodwort? That is also good to stop bleeding."

"We have enough of everything to last until spring. This is a good place to set up our camp for the winter. The river is not far, and it has small waterfalls that should keep from freezing. That will keep our water fresh and cold. We know that the hunting around here is good. There are many large animals and more small animals that we can trap. A few deadfalls set up on the game trails should provide us with many animals for food, clothing and shelter."

Chamois stood there watching the commotion and silently wondered how they all knew what to do without being told what to do. "We have found them, but no one has made us welcome. No

193

one has talked to us since we attacked that beast called the terrible one. I do not want to stay here if we are not wanted. Let's go and try to find our way back to our band."

Lifting her traveling pack back onto her shoulders, Mountain Goat turned toward the edge of the tree line. "You are right, not one person in the clan has talked to us since we helped kill that great killer of all that walks."

Moon glanced up from where she was letting her newborn baby suckle at her breast. "Where are you going?" she called out, as Chamois and Mountain Goat moved closer to the edge of the field where they were camping. "You should not be so close to where the fire doesn't show any danger."

"We are going," Chamois said softly.

"Going?" Ibex yelled, from where she was talking to Gesher and Fawn. "No, stay! We have not had a single heartbeat to talk and to thank you for helping kill the terrible one. We do not know who you are or where you came from. Come, sit, eat and talk."

Mountain Goat looked at her mate and shrugged her shoulders. "What do you think?"

Lynx ran over to where Chamois and his mate were standing and began to try to pull them back toward the middle of the encampment. "Are you leaving without saying anything? No, you are staying here with us. Your spears helped kill the terrible one. You are welcome in the Clan of Ibex. I am Lynx son of Ibex and Gesher. I welcome you to the campfires of the clan. Come, sit and share our fires and our food."

"We will stay. The winter, that is the word isn't it for when the snow and cold makes us stay inside our shelters, is starting to send us signs that soon the storms will come?"

"Yes, the word is winter and the high peaks are already becoming covered with the first snow of the winter."

Gesher clasped the man on the shoulder and then gave him a massive squeeze. "It is my fault that you were not made as welcome as you should have been. The excitement of the kill of the terrible one and then the birth of the baby made us forget that clans must make strangers welcome and invite them to their fires for a feast. The clan of Ibex welcomes you and your family. Join us for a feast and then help us set up a winter camp."

"We will stay, it is good to find you. We have been searching for the clan of Ibex for many moons. My mate and little girl are tired of the constant travel and danger."

Gesher nodded as he looked at the woman and little girl. "What did you say your names were?"

"I am called Chamois, my mate is Mountain Goat and the girl is Star."

"I remember those names from the days when we stayed to help your people who were sick from drinking the bad water. You are welcome, here and please plan on joining our clan for as long as you want."

"Those two young boys were very brave when the terrible one attacked. They both were fighting with spears to kill the predator."

"They are young, but it is the way of The Chosen. We teach them that it is something that must be done. It is either kill them or they will kill you."

"What are their names? I would like to grasp their hand."

"One is Badger and the other is Ox. But it looks like your daughter is already making Badger a friend. She just gave him a big squeeze and is not letting go."

Chamois turned around and saw his young daughter holding Badger's hand in hers as her other hand draped itself over his broad muscular shoulder. "She is making a friend, isn't she?"

"How old is she?"

Chamois shrugged his shoulders and shook his head from side to side. "Not old enough to take a mate, if that is what you are thinking. No definitely not old enough to do that."

"What, take a mate? No, that is not what I was asking. My son is barely a young boy. It will be at least seven or more seasons of new growth before I find him a mate."

Chamois nodded his head up and down. "I agree that he and she are young, and that it will be many birthing seasons before she can be mated. But we could consider a pairing between them. He seems to be a male that I would like to see mated to my daughter."

"Agreed, it is something to think about. But I would need to talk to my mate about it."

14

"Are you sure that you want to do it?"

"Star and I have talked about it since we were old enough to become a mated pair," Badger said, quietly to his mother. "We spend many nights at our hearth talking very quietly about what Star wants to do."

"But what do you want to do?"

"I want to go and explore back toward the east. Star wants to go and find new places that are north."

Star looked up from where she was rolling their sleeping skins into traveling rolls. "I have learned many things since Chamois, Mountain Goat and I joined your clan. The hardest to understand was the way that all of you feel about the other people in your clan. Once I was able to understand, I knew that it was for the best."

"I don't understand," the older woman said as she squatted down next to her son's mate. "What are you talking about?"

"The way that you talk to each other, the constant talking until both, or even more people, of the people talking understand what is being said. Then how the people that were disagreeing find some way to agree."

"It is our way, the way that the clan of Ibex does what must be done."

"And that is what we do," Badger said, as he cradled his mother in his arms. "We talk, we disagree, we talk, we disagree, we talk then we agree." He took a deep breath then looked deeply into her eyes.

"After talking and disagreeing, then talking again, we have agreed on what we are going to do. We are going toward the place where the Sun Spirit wakes in the morning. But we are also going to follow rivers and streams that come from the north. We agreed to explore both north and east."

Fawn took her son's hands in hers and kissed him on the cheek. "From the first sunrise after Chamois, Mountain Goat and Star helped kill The Terrible One, I knew you were destined to be mates. She found you and claimed you as the one she was taking as her mate."

"Claimed me?" Badger said, as he glanced over his shoulder at his mate. "How could she have claimed me? I am a male of The Chosen. I do what I want."

Star laughed that special laugh that drove Badger to the edge of desire. It seemed to be the one thing, among many that she did, that made him love her. "Your mother is right. From the first heartbeat that I saw you attacking The Terrible One I knew you were the male for me. Don't ask how I knew or how I made you want me, but it is something that we, the females of The Chosen and even The Second People know in our hearts."

"But," he started to ask, then saw Fawn shaking her head.

"Your mate is right, how it happens only the spirits know. But it is what any woman, even a young girl like Star was when she and her father and mother joined our clan, knows. She was young, barely a young girl, but she knew."

Badger and Star stood on the edge of a large cliff that was overlooking the other side of the wide river and gazed at the towering pines that covered the whole bank.

"If we are to get down there and cross the river, we have to get down this cliff," Star whispered softly and took Badger's hand. "It is nearly straight down."

Badger felt her hand in his and squeezed it feeling her fingers slip between his. "We have to look for a way to get down from here if we are going to cross the river and follow the stream that flows into it on the other side of the river."

"There is no way to cross the river back the way we came," Star said, and shuddered slightly listening to the roaring of the torrent as it flowed between the constricting sides of the river banks.

"No, we have to continue upstream and look for a way down from here. There is no way we can get down from here," Badger said, as his eyes searched for a way, any way, down off the precipice.

Star slowly placed her one foot onto the large rock outcropping. As she felt the firm surface of the massive boulder under her toes she paused, then stepped boldly onto the rough face of the largest rock on the edge of the abyss. "You have to see this!" Her shout was almost drowned out by the tumult of the surging water as it forced itself between the narrow confines of the tall cliffs on both sides.

The raging river was slowly being constricted between the sides of the gorge. As it continued its winding torturous travel toward the ocean, the river had to contend with the thick unyielding canyon walls that forced it to meander in a serpentine direction. First it went south, then nearly west before again turning south, then agonizingly back toward the west. It even was forced backward as it curled through the impervious rock and flowed north for a short distance, before again switching direction and resuming its journey toward the southwest. It surged over small outcroppings and dropped down into swirling pools causing tiny whirlpools at the base of the falls.

Star stood on the outcropping and watched the torrent of foam flecked water fight its way past the boulders strewn in a haphazard manor as if the spirits had held them in their hands and then just tossed them in the river without thinking about how they would land. "What were the spirits thinking when they made this place?"

"I don't know," Badger said, in a voice that strained to be heard.

"I think that I can see a way down," Star signed, as she gave up trying to talk.

"Where?" Badger signaled back, as his eyes searched the nearly perpendicular side of the precipice. "I can't see anything that looks like a trail."

"Not a trail, no animal, not even a mountain goat or a chamois would make a trail down the side of this dangerous rock face. But I do think that I can make out a path of some kind that I could follow. It is not a real path, but some of the rocks are flatter then the others. If I, or we, are very careful where we step I think that we can get down to the river."

"Then what?" Badger asked, as he dropped to a knee and crept closer to the edge. "Once we are down there, where do we go?"

Star looked at the river, then at her mate, then the sheer face of the rock where they were standing. "I don't know."

"If we get down there, I know that there is no way we could get back up. We would be committed to following the river upstream and I don't like the narrow steep cliffs that are on both sides. We could be trapped with no way to escape."

"You're right, it would be foolish to try to get down and then have no way to get back up. We have already come too far upstream to have to backtrack to find a way back up to the rim."

"We could stop following the river and start going north through the forest."

"But that would take us into the high peaks."

"High peaks are just what keeps the valleys separate. Valleys are always on the other side of the mountain peaks."

"Some are even hidden in the middle of the peaks between two or three mountains."

"So are you saying we should stop following the river and go into the forest?"

"Yes, that is what I am saying. I want to go north and away from this river."

"Then that is what I want to do. This constant noise from the river is starting to make me nervous. It is so loud that it would be impossible to hear any carnivore coming to attack us."

"It is dangerous to travel where you can't hear an attack coming until it is too late."

Star stirred in her sleeping skins and reached over to where Badger was sleeping. Her hand brushed his large firm muscular thigh and she rolled closer. His musky scent filled her nostrils as she snuggled against his back and again fell asleep.

As the Sun Spirit started to slowly rise over the horizon a gentle mist formed in the morning air and the barely noticeable droplets gently fell on Star's bare shoulder and neck. Twisting slightly in her sleeping skins, she pulled the thick coverings up and over her shoulders as she snuggled closer to Badger.

Suddenly she sat straight up letting the skins slip from her shoulders. "Badger, wake up!"

His spear was clenched in his one hand and his club in the other before his eyes were even fully awake. "What is it?" His whisper made her realize that he thought that there was danger.

"I'm sorry that I startled you," she said softly, and leaned over and kissed him. "But have you noticed?"

"What?" he asked, as he let the spear and club fall to the ground.

"No sound, nothing, it is quiet."

He paused as he realized what she had said. For the first morning since they had started following the river there was no sound of the rushing current. "I don't hear the river! We have traveled far enough so that the river no longer can be heard."

"The silence is beautiful, I was so used to the constant noise of the river that I didn't know when the sound stopped. If we don't hear it now, we did not hear it last night when we stopped to sleep. But we didn't realize that the silence had replaced the sound."

"I agree," Badger replied as he pulled her toward him and kissed her. "Now, how about making the morning even more special?"

"I want you to make love to me like you did the first night we were mates. I want to make this morning special also. I have been thinking of something, but the constant noise of the river as we traveled along the banks made it hard to talk and tell you what I think is happening."

"Something is happening?" Badger said, as his arms enfolded her. "What is happening, is it something good or is it something bad?"

"It is good, I am happy it happened!" Star said, as her hands slid under his skins groping for his manhood.

"What is it woman? Tell me so that I will know."

"It has been seven moons since we became mates."

"I know that, the Moon Spirit has shown us her full face seven times. It has been five moons since we started out alone on our journey."

202

"And it has been three moons since The Spirit of All Women made me bleed. When a female does not bleed for three moons it means she is expecting."

Badger stood there for a few heartbeats as what she had said to him made him think. His mate was expecting. There was a baby growing in her belly.

"We have to find a place to make a camp. If you are expecting, we can no longer continue to travel. It is not safe."

"What are you saying? Of course we can. The baby will not come for many more moons. We can travel for many more moons. I will let you know when we have to seek a place for a camp to stay for a few moons."

"But we are alone. There are no other women here. I think we should seek other clans, or even a band of The Second People, so that we have other people around us."

"It will be fine. I am young and strong. Females have had babies alone while their mates hunted. It is the way of The Chosen. We do what must be done. When the day of the birth is coming, I will tell you. But for now the baby in my belly and I will be fine." Star pulled her mate on top of her and her tongue probed his open mouth. "Now make love to me."

Badger paused for a heartbeat as he gazed at her face. "Woman," he muttered softly as his hands caressed her breast, "I love you, and I will love the baby growing in your belly."

"I hope so," Star said, and looked over at the Sun Spirit now topping the trees and shining onto the open field where they were camped. "I am expecting," she again said, "I am expecting!

"Will it be a boy or a girl?" Badger asked. Then answered before she could. "Only the spirits know, but boy or girl is not importan'

I will teach our son or daughter to survive and to hunt. I will show him or her what is needed to live."

"We will teach our child!" Star said, glancing at him out of the side of her eyes to keep the bright sunlight out of her eyes. "We both will show him or her what is needed to live, to survive and to enjoy what is done."

THE END